THE 20th Century Children's Book Treasury

Celebrated Picture Books and Stories to Read Aloud

selected by JANET SCHULMAN

Alfred A. Knopf · New York

For my two best mentors—
my daughter, Nicole Morgan Schulman,
and my friend and editor, Susan Hirschman

THIS IS A BORZOI BOOK PUBLISHED BY ALFRED A. KNOPF, INC.

Compilation copyright © 1998 by Janet Schulman.
Cover, title page, and front-matter illustrations copyright © 1998 by Kevin Henkes.
All rights reserved under International and Pan-American Copyright Conventions. Published in the United States by
Alfred A. Knopf, Inc., New York, and simultaneously in Canada by Random House of Canada Limited, Toronto.
Distributed by Random House, Inc., New York.

Book design by Roberta Pressel
Hand-lettering by Bernard Maisner
Acknowledgments for permission to reproduce previously published material appear on page 308.

www.randomhouse.com/kids/

Library of Congress Cataloging-in-Publication Data
The 20th-century children's book treasury : celebrated picture books and stories
to read aloud / compiled by Janet Schulman.
p. cm.
Summary: A collection of picture-book stories by such authors as Ludwig Bemelmans,
Ezra Jack Keats, and Maurice Sendak.
ISBN 0-679-88647-8
1. Children's stories. [1. Short stories.] I. Schulman, Janet.
PZ5.A127   1998
[E]—dc21   98-12870

Printed in the United States of America
10 9 8 7 6 5 4

CONTENTS

A NOTE TO PARENTS

As every mother or father knows, abiding by all the rules that define a "good" parent is a Herculean task. In 1968, when my daughter was born, reading books to one's child was not yet universally recognized as one of those written-in-stone "good parent" responsibilities. But I, like millions before and after me, somehow knew that sharing a book with a young child who's cuddled up next to you is one of the nicest rewards of parenting. It was not a task, Herculean or otherwise; it was fun.

Since then, the many educational and emotional benefits of reading to the preschool-age child have been demonstrated in numerous scientific studies. A few years ago, a group of Boston pediatricians deemed this activity so important in the development of the whole child that they began distributing free books at their clinic. This in turn helped spark the White House's nationwide "America Reads" initiative. After nearly forty years of working in the children's book publishing industry, I find it gratifying to see that more and more Americans understand that books help give children a leg up on the ladder of life.

The picture books and stories that I have selected for this anthology are all personal favorites of mine; the majority are also the tried-and-true favorites of millions of others. Included are four books that were awarded the Caldecott Medal by the American Library Association as "the most distinguished American picture book for children" in the year of their publication and eight runners-up (Caldecott Honor Books), as well as many other award-winning books. With the exception of one story, which I will discuss later, all of the selections were written and illustrated in the twentieth century.

This was the century during which children's books, and most especially the picture book, came to fruition. Starting in 1919, in response to the rapid expansion of the free public library system, American publishers began establishing children's book departments. At the same time, new printing technologies made it possible to manufacture beautiful books at affordable prices. And then after World War II came the baby boom, and with it a vastly expanded audience for children's books. Without those developments, it seems unlikely that we would have such a rich array of children's books today.

The selections in this book present an overview of the authors and illustrators who have shaped children's picture books during this century. I have had the good fortune of living with many of these books, from my childhood in the 1930s through my continuing work with children's books as an editor and writer. The very first book I remember owning, though I am sure there were earlier ones that have faded from memory, was *The Story of Ferdinand*. It was given to me on my third birthday and it had just been published. How I loved that bull who preferred sniffing the flowers to fighting! Ferdinand is now in his sixties and still captivating the imagination of children throughout the world. Really good stories—*Millions of Cats, Mike Mulligan and His Steam Shovel, Make Way for Ducklings*, to name a few of the older gems in this anthology—do that. And if some of the illustrations look "old-fashioned" to us adults, remember that a child comes to every book with fresh eyes.

Sometimes, however, beloved books of an earlier age can offend and hurt. The transformation of *The Story of Little Black Sambo*, originally published in 1899 and the only story in this anthology written before the turn of the century, into *The Story of Little Babaji*, published in 1996, is a triumph in finding an authentic way to preserve the best of a long-time favorite story.

Helen Bannerman, the author and illustrator of the original book, lived in India when she wrote this tale about tigers who chased each other so furiously that they turned into a pool of "ghi," an Indian word for melted butter. Unfortunately, the names she gave her characters and her amateurish illustrations depicted them as gross stereotypes of Africans. Millions of children in America grew up with this story until mid-century, when American librarians, both black and white, made us realize how offensive the illustrations were. I have closed this anthology with *The Story of Little Babaji*, in which Fred Marcellino has given Mrs. Bannerman's characters real Indian names and created beautiful new illustrations that are clearly set in India. Thus a wonderful story, nearly one hundred years old, has been given a new life for all children.

Almost every child has a favorite book—really, a favorite character, be it human or animal—that they never grow tired of hearing. To my daughter, the rebellious little boy, Max, who sailed his boat to *Where the Wild Things Are*, was totally real. "Hi, Max!" she used to call from our window overlooking the Hudson River whenever a sailboat went by. And I have heard of children who, when visiting France, are interested only in seeing fearless Madeline's "old house in Paris that was covered with vines" and its "twelve little girls in two straight lines." Curious George, Frog and Toad, and Frances are some of the other classic story-book characters children will make lifelong friends with in this book. I am not clairvoyant, but I feel fairly certain that fifty years from now some of the characters from the more recently published books in this anthology will be included along with the beloved favorites I've mentioned.

With two exceptions (*Amelia Bedelia* and *Petunia*, which were abridged slightly), all of the selections include the entire original text. Each story is presented on the oversized pages with an eye to capturing the spirit of the original book. Thus this anthology is designed to function as a comfortable lap book to be read and shared with the children in your family. Older children who have learned to read will also enjoy reading some of their favorites to themselves or to their younger siblings. But once reading aloud has become a habit in your family, even school-age children who are good readers will want to have you read to them from time to time, and, chances are, you will want to!

Because children are not little robots, all on the same programmed course of development, there is no pretested way to know precisely which stories a child will most enjoy at a particular age. However, to help parents who have not had a lot of trial-and-error experience in selecting books for children, we have placed a color-coded symbol with each story to indicate the approximate age level.

This red book at the bottom of the page indicates a story for the youngest child. These range from Helen Oxenbury's *I Hear, I See,* and *I Touch* and other early-learning concept books for babies and toddlers to wonderfully simple stories such as Margaret Wise Brown's *Goodnight Moon* and Peggy Rathmann's *Good Night, Gorilla.* These are what we often call "see and say" books, in which the reader helps the toddler learn the names of objects and animals by pointing to the pictures and saying what they are called.

This blue book represents the next step up, and herein lies the heart of the true preschool picture book: a narrative story told with few words (sometimes no words) and many pictures. The span of childhood experiences displayed in these picture books is vast, from Ezra Jack Keats's celebration of *The Snowy Day* to Kevin Henkes's saga of *Owen,* the boy who would not give up his security blanket.

Longer stories that are told primarily with words, such as Judith Viorst's *Alexander and the Terrible, Horrible, No Good, Very Bad Day* or the adventures of Winnie-the-Pooh, are indicated with this green book. They often require a greater attention span or a range of experience that is most frequently found in children over five years of age.

As you begin using this book with children, you will soon become your own best judge of which stories are right for your child now and which ones your child will grow into. If your child falls in love with one of the stories and must hear it night after night after night, consider purchasing the original book. It will be easier to tote to nursery school, the playground, or Grandma's—and thirty years from now it will be a cherished childhood memento.

While I believe that the selections in this book are among the best from the twentieth century, there are other books that certainly deserve to be called "best" also. To publish this book at an affordable price, it was necessary to limit the number of selections, and I have selected only books whose integrity would not be compromised when the illustrations were reduced to fit the format. Biographical notes about each of the authors and illustrators, starting on page 298, include some of the other excellent books by them. But it is really my hope that the pleasure this collection brings you and your family will motivate you to visit your library or bookstore more often and become a children's book expert in your own right, discovering authors and illustrators not represented here and always being on the lookout for someone new and good.

In closing, I would like to thank Simon Boughton, publishing director of Alfred A. Knopf Books for Young Readers, for asking me to compile this anthology and, along with Sarah Morgan, for giving me so much help in seeing it through. Special thanks also to Pat Buckley at HarperCollins and Regina Hayes at Viking for their early support of this project and to all the publishers who followed by granting permission to include their books.

Here's wishing that you have as much fun reading and looking at *The 20th-Century Children's Book Treasury* as I had putting it together.

—Janet Schulman
September 1998

THE 20th Century Children's Book Treasury

MADELINE

Written and illustrated by Ludwig Bemelmans

Originally published in 1939

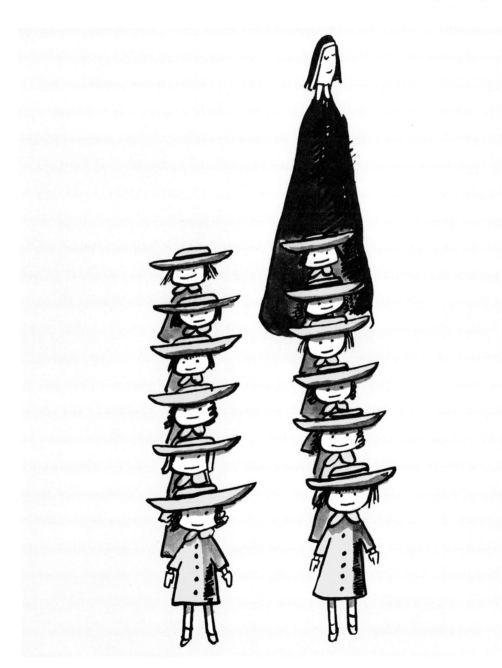

In an old house in Paris
that was covered with vines
lived twelve little girls in two straight lines.

  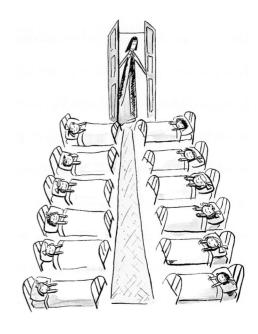

In two straight lines
they broke their bread

and brushed their teeth

and went to bed.

They smiled at the good

and frowned at the bad

and sometimes they were very sad.

They left the house
at half past nine
in two straight lines

in rain

or shine—

the smallest one was Madeline.

She was not afraid of mice—

she loved winter, snow, and ice.
To the tiger in the zoo
Madeline just said, "Pooh-pooh,"

and nobody knew so well
how to frighten Miss Clavel.

In the middle of one night
Miss Clavel turned on her light
and said, "Something is not right!"

Little Madeline sat in bed,
cried and cried; her eyes were red.

And soon after Dr. Cohn
came, he rushed out to the phone
and he dialed: DANton-ten-six—

"Nurse," he said, "it's an appendix!"

Everybody had to cry—
not a single eye was dry.
Madeline was in his arm
in a blanket safe and warm.
In a car with a red light
they drove out into the night.

Madeline woke up two hours later, in a room with flowers. Madeline soon ate and drank. On her bed there was a crank,

and a crack on the ceiling had the habit of sometimes looking like a rabbit.

Outside were birds, trees, and sky— and so ten days passed quickly by.

One nice morning Miss Clavel said— "Isn't this a fine—

day to visit

Madeline."

VISITORS FROM TWO TO FOUR
read a sign outside her door

Tiptoeing with solemn face,
with some flowers and a vase,

in they walked and then said, "Ahhh,"
when they saw the toys and candy
and the dollhouse from Papa.

But the biggest surprise by far—
on her stomach
was a scar!

"Good-by," they said, "we'll come again,"

and the little girls left in the rain.

They went home
and broke their bread

brushed their teeth

and went to bed.

In the middle of the night
Miss Clavel turned on the light
and said, "Something is not right!"

And afraid of a disaster

Miss Clavel ran fast
and faster,

and she said, "Please children do—
tell me what is troubling you?"

And all the little girls cried, "Boohoo,
we want to have our appendix out, too!"

"Good night, little girls!
Thank the lord you are well!
And now go to sleep!"
said Miss Clavel.
    And she turned out the light—
        and closed the door—
            and that's all there is—
                there isn't any more.

14

CHICKA CHICKA BOOM BOOM

Written by Bill Martin, Jr., and John Archambault
Illustrated by Lois Ehlert

Originally published in 1989

A told B,
and B told C,
"I'll meet you at the top
of the coconut tree."

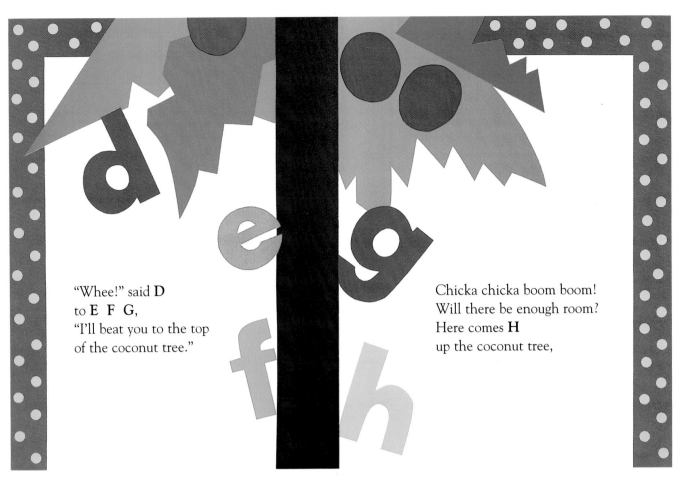

"Whee!" said **D**
to **E F G**,
"I'll beat you to the top
of the coconut tree."

Chicka chicka boom boom!
Will there be enough room?
Here comes **H**
up the coconut tree,

and **I** and **J**
and tag-along **K**,
all on their way
up the coconut tree.

Chicka chicka boom boom!
Will there be enough room?
Look who's coming!
L M N O P!

And **Q R** S!

And **T U V**!

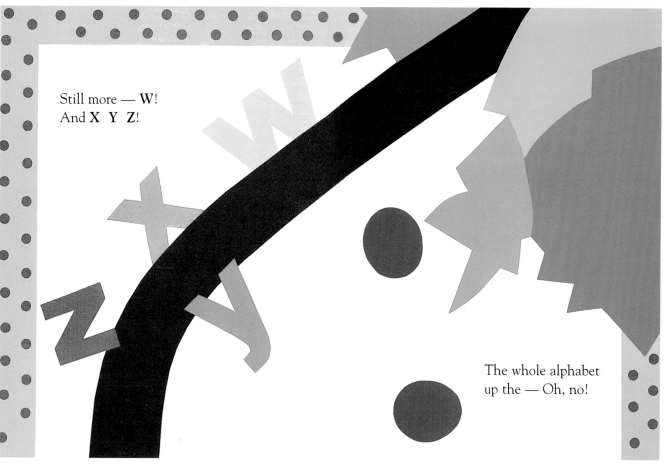

Still more — **W**!
And **X Y Z**!

The whole alphabet
up the — Oh, no!

Chicka chicka . . .
BOOM!
BOOM!

Skit skat skoodle doot.
Flip flop flee.
Everybody running to the coconut tree.
Mamas and papas
and uncles and aunts
hug their little dears,
then dust their pants.

"Help us up," cried **A B C**.

Next from the pileup
skinned-knee **D**
and stubbed-toe **E**
and patched-up **F**.
Then comes **G**
all out of breath.

H is tangled up with **I**.
J and **K** are about to cry.
L is knotted like a tie.

M is looped.
N is stooped.
O is twisted alley-oop.
Skit skat skoodle doot.
Flip flop flee.

Look who's coming!
It's black-eyed **P**,
Q R S,
and loose-tooth **T**.

Then **U V W**
wiggle-jiggle free.

Last to come
X Y Z.
And the sun goes down
on the coconut tree...

But—
chicka chicka boom boom!
Look, there's a full moon.

A is out of bed,
and this is what he said,
"Dare double dare,
you can't catch me.
I'll beat you to the top
of the coconut tree."
Chicka chicka
BOOM! BOOM!

SWIMMY

Written and illustrated by Leo Lionni

Originally published in 1963

A happy school of little fish lived in a corner of the sea somewhere.
They were all red. Only one of them was as black as a mussel shell.
He swam faster than his brothers and sisters. His name was Swimmy.

One bad day a tuna fish, swift,
fierce and very hungry, came darting
through the waves. In one gulp he
swallowed all the little red fish.
Only Swimmy escaped.

He swam away in the deep wet world. He was scared, lonely and very sad.

But the sea was full of wonderful creatures, and as he swam from marvel to marvel Swimmy was happy again.

He saw a medusa made of rainbow jelly . . .
a lobster, who walked about like a water-moving machine . . .
strange fish, pulled by an invisible thread . . .
a forest of seaweeds growing from sugar-candy rocks . . .
an eel whose tail was almost too far away to remember . . .
and sea anemones, who looked like pink palm trees swaying in the wind.

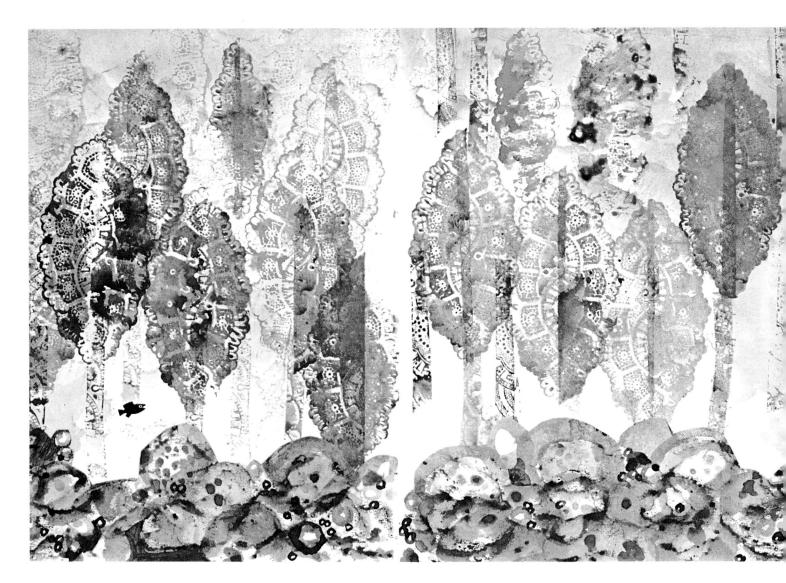

Then, hidden in the dark shade of rocks and weeds, he saw a school of little fish, just like his own.

"Let's go and swim and play and SEE things!" he said happily.

"We can't," said the little red fish. "The big fish will eat us all."

"But you can't just lie there," said Swimmy. "We must THINK of something."

Swimmy thought and thought and thought.

Then suddenly he said, "I have it! We are going to swim all together like the biggest fish in the sea!"

He taught them to swim close together, each in his own place,

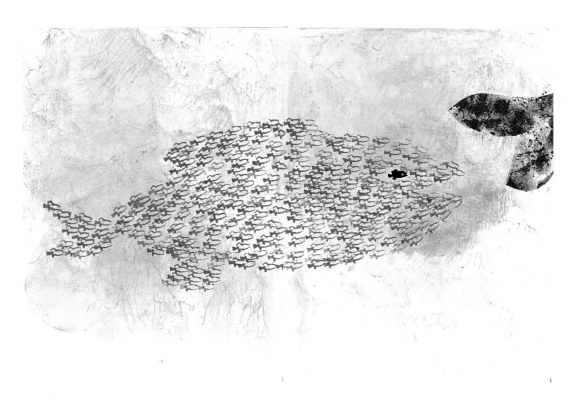

and when they had learned to swim like one giant fish, he said, "I'll be the eye."

And so they swam in the cool morning water and in the midday sun and chased the big fish away.

A CHAIR FOR MY MOTHER

Written and illustrated by Vera B. Williams

Originally published in 1982

My mother works as a waitress in the Blue Tile Diner. After school sometimes I go to meet her there. Then her boss Josephine gives me a job too.

I wash the salts and peppers and fill the ketchups. One time I peeled all the onions for the onion soup. When I finish, Josephine says, "Good work, honey," and pays me. And every time, I put half of my money into the jar.

It takes a long time to fill a jar this big. Every day when my mother comes home from work, I take down the jar. My mama empties all her change from tips out of her purse for me to count. Then we push all of the coins into the jar.

Sometimes my mama is laughing when she comes home from work. Sometimes she's so tired she falls asleep while I count the money out into piles. Some days she has lots of tips. Some days she has only a little. Then she looks worried. But each evening every single shiny coin goes into the jar.

We sit in the kitchen to count the tips. Usually Grandma sits with us too. While we count, she likes to hum. Often she has money in her old leather wallet for us. Whenever she gets a good bargain on tomatoes or bananas or something she buys, she puts by the savings and they go into the jar.

When we can't get a single other coin into the jar, we are going to take out all the money and go and buy a chair.

Yes, a chair. A wonderful, beautiful, fat, soft armchair. We will get one covered in velvet with roses all over it. We are going to get the best chair in the whole world.

That is because our old chairs burned up. There was a big fire in our other house. All our chairs burned. So did our sofa and so did everything else. That wasn't such a long time ago.

My mother and I were coming home from buying new shoes. I had new sandals. She had new pumps. We were walking to our house from the bus. We were looking at everyone's tulips. She was saying she liked red tulips and I was saying I liked yellow ones. Then we came to our block.

Right outside our house stood two big fire engines. I could see lots of smoke. Tall orange flames came out of the roof. All the neighbors stood in a bunch across the street. Mama grabbed my hand and we ran. My uncle Sandy saw us and ran to us. Mama yelled, "Where's Mother?" I yelled, "Where's my grandma?" My aunt Ida waved and shouted, "She's here, she's here. She's O.K. Don't worry."

Grandma was all right. Our cat was safe too, though it took a while to find her. But everything else in our house was spoiled.

What was left of the house was turned to charcoal and ashes.

We went to stay with my mother's sister Aunt Ida and Uncle Sandy. Then we were able to move into the apartment downstairs. We painted the walls yellow. The floors were all shiny. But the rooms were very empty.

The first day we moved in, the neighbors brought pizza and cake and ice cream. And they brought a lot of other things too.

The family across the street brought a table and three kitchen chairs. The very old man next door gave us a bed from when his children were little.

My other grandpa brought us his beautiful rug. My mother's other sister, Sally, had made us red and white curtains. Mama's boss, Josephine, brought pots and pans, silverware and dishes. My cousin brought me her own stuffed bear.

Everyone clapped when my grandma made a speech. "You are all the kindest people," she said, "and we thank you very, very much. It's lucky we're young and can start all over."

That was last year, but we still have no sofa and no big chairs. When Mama comes home, her feet hurt. "There's no good place for me to take a load off my feet," she says. When Grandma wants to sit back and hum and cut up potatoes, she has to get as comfortable as she can on a hard kitchen chair.

So that is how come Mama brought home the biggest jar she could find at the diner and all the coins started to go into the jar.

Now the jar is too heavy for me to lift down. Uncle Sandy gave me a quarter. He had to boost me up so I could put it in.

After supper Mama and Grandma and I stood in front of the jar. "Well, I never would have believed it, but I guess it's full," Mama said.

My mother brought home little paper wrappers for the nickels and the dimes and the quarters. I counted them all out and wrapped them all up.

On my mother's day off, we took all the coins to the bank. The bank exchanged them for ten-dollar bills. Then we took the bus downtown to shop for our chair.

We shopped through four furniture stores. We tried out big chairs and smaller ones, high chairs and low chairs, soft chairs and harder ones. Grandma said she felt like Goldilocks in "The Three Bears" trying out all the chairs.

Finally we found the chair we were all dreaming of. And the money in the jar was enough to pay for it. We called Aunt Ida and Uncle Sandy. They came right down in their pickup truck to drive the chair home for us. They knew we couldn't wait for it to be delivered.

I tried out our chair in the back of the truck. Mama wouldn't let me sit there while we drove. But they let me sit in it while they carried it up to the door.

We set the chair right beside the window with the red and white curtains. Grandma and Mama and I all sat in it while Aunt Ida took our picture.

Now Grandma sits in it and talks with people going by in the daytime. Mama sits down and watches the news on TV when she comes home from her job. After supper, I sit with her and she can reach right up and turn out the light if I fall asleep in her lap.

GOODNIGHT MOON

Written by Margaret Wise Brown
Illustrated by Clement Hurd

Originally published in 1947

In the great green room
There was a telephone
And a red balloon
And a picture of—

The cow jumping over the moon

And there were three little bears
sitting on chairs

And two little kittens
And a pair of mittens

And a little toyhouse
And a young mouse

And a comb and a brush
and a bowl full of mush

And a quiet old lady
who was whispering "hush"

Goodnight room

Goodnight moon

Goodnight cow jumping over the moon

Goodnight light
And the red balloon

Goodnight bears
Goodnight chairs

Goodnight kittens

And goodnight mittens

Goodnight clocks
And goodnight socks

Goodnight little house

And goodnight mouse

Goodnight comb
And goodnight brush

Goodnight nobody   Goodnight mush

And goodnight to the old lady
whispering "hush"

Goodnight stars   Goodnight air

Goodnight noises everywhere

THE SNOWY DAY

Written and illustrated by Ezra Jack Keats

Originally published in 1962

One winter morning Peter woke up and
looked out the window. Snow had fallen during
the night. It covered everything as far as he
could see.

After breakfast he put on his snowsuit and ran outside. The snow was piled up very high along the street to make a path for walking.

Crunch, crunch, crunch, his feet sank into the snow.

He walked with his toes pointing out, like this:

He walked with his toes pointing in, like that:

Then he dragged his feet s-l-o-w-l-y to make tracks.
And he found something sticking out of the snow that made a new track.

It was a stick—a stick that was just right for smacking a snow-covered tree.

Down fell the snow—plop!— on top of Peter's head.

He thought it would be fun to join the big boys in their snowball fight, but he knew he wasn't old enough—not yet.

So he made a smiling snowman, and he made angels.

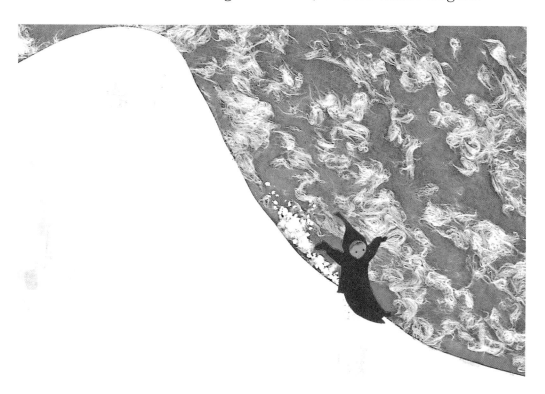

He pretended he was a mountain-climber. He climbed up a great big tall heaping mountain of snow—and slid all the way down.

He picked up a handful of snow—and another, and still another. He packed it round and firm and put the snowball in his pocket for tomorrow. Then he went into his warm house.

He told his mother all about his adventures while she took off his wet socks.

And he thought and thought and thought about them.

Before he got into bed he looked in his pocket. His pocket was empty. The snowball wasn't there. He felt very sad.

While he slept, he dreamed that the sun had melted all the snow away.

But when he woke up his dream was gone. The snow was still everywhere. New snow was falling!

After breakfast he called to his friend from across the hall, and they went out together into the deep, deep snow.

THE LETTER
(from FROG AND TOAD ARE FRIENDS)

Written and illustrated by Arnold Lobel

Originally published in 1970

Toad was sitting on his front porch.
Frog came along and said,
"What is the matter, Toad?
You are looking sad."
"Yes," said Toad.
"This is my sad time of day.
It is the time
when I wait for the mail to come.
It always makes me very unhappy."
"Why is that?" asked Frog.

"Because I never get any mail,"
said Toad.
"Not ever?" asked Frog.
"No, never," said Toad.
"No one has ever sent me a letter.
Every day my mailbox is empty.
That is why waiting for the mail
is a sad time for me."
Frog and Toad sat on the porch,
feeling sad together.

Then Frog said,
"I have to go home now, Toad.
There is something that I must do."
Frog hurried home.

He found a pencil
and a piece of paper.
He wrote on the paper.
He put the paper in an envelope.
On the envelope he wrote
"A LETTER FOR TOAD."
Frog ran out of his house.
He saw a snail that he knew.
"Snail," said Frog, "please take
this letter to Toad's house
and put it in his mailbox."
"Sure," said the snail. "Right away."

Then Frog ran back to Toad's house.
Toad was in bed, taking a nap.
"Toad," said Frog,
"I think you should get up
and wait for the mail some more."
"No," said Toad,
"I am tired of waiting for the mail."

Frog looked out of the window
at Toad's mailbox.
The snail was not there yet.
"Toad," said Frog, "you never know
when someone may send you a letter."
"No, no," said Toad. "I do not think
anyone will ever send me a letter."
Frog looked out of the window.
The snail was not there yet.
"But, Toad," said Frog,
"someone may send you a letter today."
"Don't be silly," said Toad.
"No one has ever sent me
a letter before, and no one
will send me a letter today."

Frog looked out of the window.
The snail was still not there.
"Frog, why do you keep looking
out of the window?" asked Toad.
"Because now I am waiting
for the mail," said Frog.
"But there will not be any," said Toad.
"Oh, yes there will," said Frog,
"because I have sent you a letter."

They sat there,
feeling happy together.
Frog and Toad waited a long time.
Four days later
the snail got to Toad's house
and gave him the letter from Frog.
Toad was very pleased to have it.

"You have?" said Toad.
"What did you write in the letter?"
Frog said, "I wrote
'Dear Toad, I am glad
that you are my best friend.
Your best friend, Frog.' "
"Oh," said Toad,
"that makes a very good letter."
Then Frog and Toad went out
onto the front porch
to wait for the mail.

FREIGHT TRAIN

Written and illustrated by Donald Crews

Originally published in 1978

A train runs across this track.

Red caboose at the back

Orange tank car next

Yellow hopper car

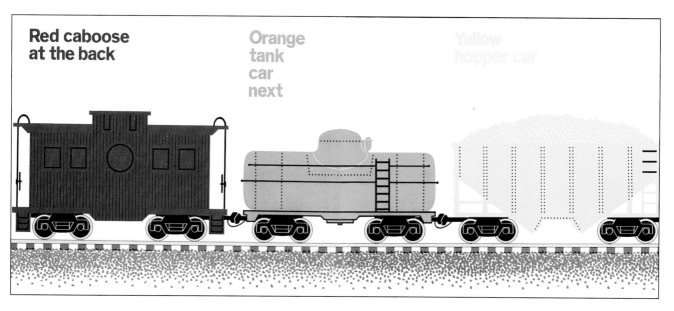

**Green
cattle car**

**Blue
gondola
car**

**Purple
box car**

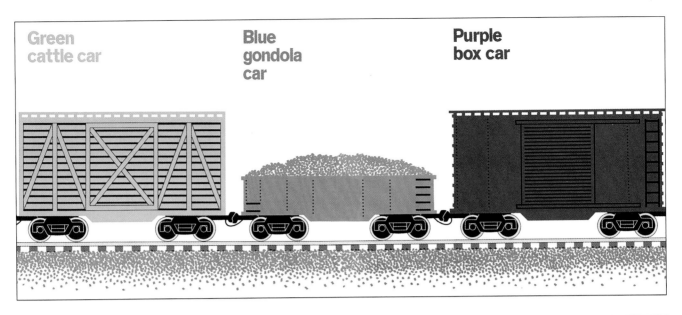

**a Black
tender and**

**a Black
steam engine.**

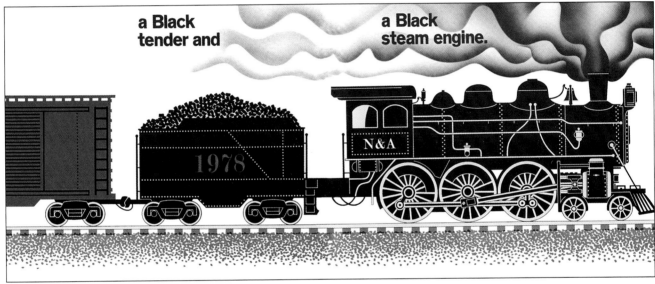

Freight train.

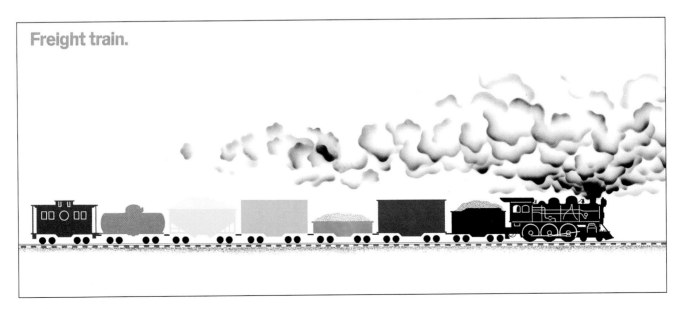

52

Moving.

Going through tunnels

Going by cities

Crossing trestles.

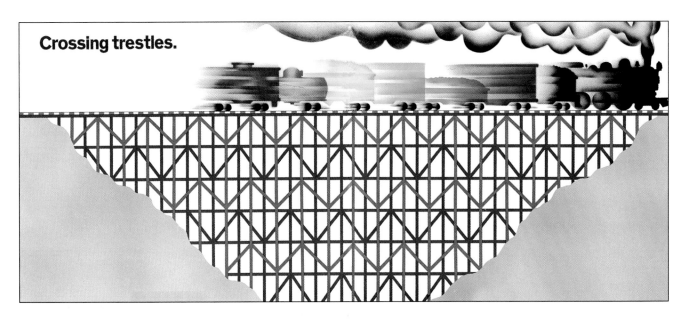

Moving in darkness. **Moving in daylight.
Going, going...**

gone.

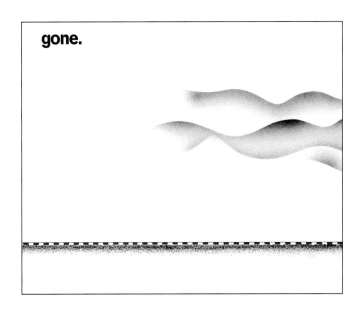

MAKE WAY FOR DUCKLINGS

Written and illustrated by Robert McCloskey

Originally published in 1941

Mr. and Mrs. Mallard were looking for a place to live. But every time Mr. Mallard saw what looked like a nice place, Mrs. Mallard said it was no good. There were sure to be foxes in the woods or turtles in the water, and she was not going to raise a family where there might be foxes or turtles. So they flew on and on.

When they got to Boston, they felt too tired to fly any further. There was a nice pond in the Public Garden, with a little island on it. "The very place to spend the night," quacked Mr. Mallard. So down they flapped.

Next morning they fished for their breakfast in the mud at the bottom of the pond. But they didn't find much.

Just as they were getting ready to start on their way, a strange enormous bird came by. It was pushing a boat full of people, and there was a man sitting on its back. "Good morning," quacked Mr. Mallard, being polite. The big bird was too proud to answer. But the people on the boat threw peanuts into the water, so the Mallards followed them all round the pond and got another breakfast, better than the first.

"I like this place," said Mrs. Mallard as they climbed out on the bank and waddled along. "Why don't we build a nest and raise our ducklings right in this pond? There are no foxes and no turtles, and the people feed us peanuts. What could be better?"

"Good," said Mr. Mallard, delighted that at last Mrs. Mallard had found a place that suited her. But—

"Look out!" squawked Mrs. Mallard, all of a dither. "You'll get run over!" And when she got her breath she added: "*This* is no place for babies, with all those horrid things rushing about. We'll have to look somewhere else."

WEEBK!

So they flew over Beacon Hill and round the State House, but there was no place there.

They looked in Louisburg Square, but there was no water to swim in.

Then they flew over the Charles River. "This is better," quacked Mr. Mallard. "That island looks like a nice quiet place, and it's only a little way from the Public Garden."

"Yes," said Mrs. Mallard, remembering the peanuts. "That looks like just the right place to hatch ducklings."

So they chose a cozy spot among the bushes near the water and settled down to build their nest. And only just in time, for now they were beginning to molt. All their old wing feathers started to drop out, and they would not be able to fly again until the new ones grew in.

But of course they could swim, and one day they swam over to the park on the river bank, and there they met a policeman called Michael. Michael fed them peanuts, and after that the Mallards called on Michael every day.

After Mrs. Mallard had laid eight eggs in the nest she couldn't go to visit Michael any more, because she had to sit on the eggs to keep them warm. She moved off the nest only to get a drink of water, or to have her lunch, or to count the eggs and make sure they were all there.

One day the ducklings hatched out. First came Jack, then Kack, and then Lack, then Mack and Nack and Ouack and Pack and Quack. Mr. and Mrs. Mallard were bursting with pride. It was a great responsibility taking care of so many ducklings, and it kept them very busy.

One day Mr. Mallard decided he'd like to take a trip to see what the rest of the river was like, further on. So off he set. "I'll meet you in a week, in the Public Garden," he quacked over his shoulder. "Take good care of the ducklings."

"Don't you worry," said Mrs. Mallard. "I know all about bringing up children." And she did.

She taught them how to swim and dive.

She taught them to walk in a line, to come when they were called, and to keep a safe distance from bikes and scooters and other things with wheels.

When at last she felt perfectly satisfied with them, she said one morning: "Come along, children. Follow me." Before you could wink an eyelash Jack, Kack, Lack, Mack, Nack, Ouack, Pack, and Quack fell into line, just as they had been taught. Mrs. Mallard led the way into the water and they swam behind her to the opposite bank.

There they waded ashore and waddled along till they came to the highway.

Mrs. Mallard stepped out to cross the road. "Honk, honk!" went the horns on the speeding cars. "Qua-a-ack!" went Mrs. Mallard as she tumbled back again. "Quack! Quack! Quack! Quack!" went Jack, Kack, Lack, Mack, Nack, Ouack, Pack, and Quack, just as loud as their little quackers could quack. The cars kept speeding by and honking, and Mrs. Mallard and the ducklings kept right on quack-quack-quacking.

They made such a noise that Michael came running, waving his arms and blowing his whistle. He planted himself in the center of the road, raised one hand to stop the traffic, and then beckoned with the other, the way policemen do, for Mrs. Mallard to cross over.

As soon as Mrs. Mallard and the ducklings were safe on the other side and on their way down Mount Vernon Street, Michael rushed back to his police booth.

He called Clancy at headquarters and said: "There's a family of ducks walkin' down the street!" Clancy said: "Family of *what?*" "*Ducks!*" yelled Michael. "Send a police car, quick!"

Meanwhile Mrs. Mallard had reached the Corner Book Shop and turned into Charles Street, with Jack, Kack, Lack, Mack, Nack, Ouack, Pack, and Quack all marching in line behind her.

Everyone stared. An old lady from Beacon Hill said: "Isn't it amazing!" and the man who swept the streets said: "Well, now, ain't that nice!" and when Mrs. Mallard heard them she was so proud she tipped her nose in the air and walked along with an extra swing in her waddle.

When they came to the corner of Beacon Street there was the police car with four policemen that Clancy had sent from head-quarters. The policemen held back the traffic so Mrs. Mallard and the ducklings could march across the street, right on into the Public Garden.

Inside the gate they all turned round to say thank you to the policemen. The policemen smiled and waved good-by.

When they reached the pond and swam
across to the little island, there was Mr. Mallard
waiting for them, just as he had promised.

The ducklings liked the new island so much
that they decided to live there. All day long they
follow the swan boats and eat peanuts.

And when night falls they swim to their little
island and go to sleep.

A MILLION FISH...MORE OR LESS

Written by Patricia C. McKissack
Illustrated by Dena Schutzer

Originally published in 1992

It was early morning on the Bayou Clapateaux. Hugh Thomas had just tossed his line into the water when Papa-Daddy and Elder Abbajon came rowing out of the gauzy river fog. They were swapping bayou tales, just like they had for years.

"Morning to you," Hugh Thomas called as they pulled up alongside the bank.

Papa-Daddy started right in. "The Elder and me was just sayin' that the Bayou Clapateaux is a mighty peculiar place.

"Take the time back in '03, me and the Elder here caught a wild turkey weighed five hundred pounds!"

Hugh Thomas's eyes filled with wonder. "That's a powerful big turkey."

Quickly Elder Abbajon took up the story, adding, "As we was marchin' that gobbler home, I spied a lantern that'd been left by Spanish conquistadores back in the year 15 and 42. And it was still burning!"

"After four hundred years!" Hugh Thomas exclaimed in amazement.

Papa-Daddy lowered his voice to a whisper. "Just when the Elder picked up that lantern, the ground commenced to quaking, and the longest, meanest cottonmouth I ever did see raised up. The thing had legs, and went to chasing us. The hounds broke and run, I got tangled up in the ropes, and that turkey got clean away."

With a quick nod, he gave the story back to Elder Abbajon. "'Bout that time, a swarm of giant mosquitoes attacked. I lost my footin' and dropped the lantern in a pool of quicksand. Might' near fell in myself. 'Course, as you can see, I didn't then, 'cause I'm here now."

Hugh Thomas studied on what the two ol' swampers had told him. Then he smiled. "Y'all are just funning—right?...Did that turkey *really* weigh five hundred pounds?"

"More or less," Papa-Daddy answered, snapping his suspenders and winking his eye.

"And was that lantern *really* over four hundred years old?"

"Give or take a year or two," Elder Abbajon answered, swattin' a mosquito.

"Was it *really* still burning?"

"Well, let's just say it was flickering a bit."

And with their tale all told, the two men rowed away.

"Remember," Papa-Daddy called just 'fore they disappeared behind the curtain of fog. "Strange things do happen on the Bayou Clapateaux."

Now Hugh Thomas was alone with only worrisome mosquitoes to keep him company. But it wasn't long before he caught three small fish.

And in the next half-hour he caught a *million* more! Big ones, little ones, all sizes. The boy was so excited he whooped with joy. "Wait 'til Papa-Daddy and Elder Abbajon see this!"

Then, loading his magnificent catch on his wagon, he turned to leave.

But without warning, two yellow eyes surfaced just above the water line. Hugh Thomas knew it was Atoo, the *grand-père* of all the alligators on Jackson's Pointe. The old gator slithered onto the bank, blocking the boy's way.

"Where do you think you will go with all our fish?" he hissed angrily.

Hugh Thomas blinked. Why, that gator was talking right out! "Th-th-these are my fish," the boy answered with an uncertain spirit.

Atoo's mean eyes took in the catch. "And what's for me and mine to eat if I let you take them all?"

Hugh Thomas considered making a run for it. But the old gator must have read his mind. "Don't even think of it," he warned, inching closer. Then he chuckled softly. "Your best chance is to figure on this. If one hundred alligators one hundred feet long can move at one hundred yards per second, how long would it take us to get from this water to you and your wagon of fish? Answer now," he hissed, moving still closer.

Not long enough for me to get away! Hugh Thomas thought. Deciding that anything was better than tangling with Atoo and all his kin, he solved the riddle by throwing a goodly amount of fish back into the bayou.

"You make the right answer," Atoo said. Then he turned and disappeared beneath the dark waters, along with the hundred other alligators who had been watching and waiting.

Hugh Thomas took a quick count, and saw he still had close to a half-million fish left. He followed the swamp path that was the quickest way to Papa-Daddy and Elder Abbajon's houseboat. Story had it that Jean Polet's pirate treasure was hidden somewhere 'mongst the cypress knees, but Hugh Thomas wasn't interested. "I've got my own treasure," he boasted.

The air grew thick, hovering over the swamp like a big smothering hand. Then the still came, a terrible kind of silence with its own sound. The boy hummed and quickened his step. Something was stalking him, closing in fast. The ghost of Jean Polet, maybe?

No! Hugh Thomas was suddenly surrounded by an army of raccoons, led by the most notorious rogue of them all—Mosley!

"By my leave!" shouted the bandit leader. "We'll be demanding a toll, li'l sir. And ye wagon of fish there will do nicely."

"Wait," Hugh Thomas cried out. "That's not fair!"

"Not fair, says he!" Mosley scoffed. "And what'll be fair to you?"

"Half, maybe?" Hugh Thomas couldn't believe he was bargaining with a band of pirate raccoons.

"Why settle on half, mate, when we can *take* it all?"

Thinking fast, Hugh Thomas suggested, "A contest? That's it! We'll have a contest of some kind."

Mosley laughed coarsely. "A contest it'll be. You win, we takes half the catch. I win, we takes it all. Mind you, that's as fair as it'll be gettin'."

The boy agreed, not knowing what to expect—swords, pistols, wrestling?

Then, to his astonishment, Mosley whistled, and two black bears appeared. Reaching beneath a huge swamp cabbage, the pirate pulled out a twenty-foot snake.

"We'll skip rope, says I!"

And so the contest began.

The bears turned and Mosley jumped.

Hugh Thomas hadn't seen such fancy footwork in all his life.

That rascal skipped so hard and so fast he was down in a pit when he finally missed on jump 5,552. His motley crew sent up a loud cheer.

But Hugh Thomas held his own—1,000...2,000...3,000...4,000...4,050. Hugh Thomas jumped and jumped and jumped...5,000. He was so tired. His legs hurt, but he jumped some more...5,550. He managed just three more jumps before missing, but it was enough to win...5,553!

Mosley was purely outdone. He went to grumbling and mumbling and swearing under his breath. But in the end he made good his word. "I takes me lickin', and now I'll be takin' me fish."

One by one, hundreds of masked bandits marched past the wagon and plucked a juicy treat. Then Mosley found the plumpest fish for himself and beckoned Hugh Thomas to hurry along.

Even though his catch was cut by half again, Hugh Thomas still felt like a winner. Moving with purpose, he passed the large cypress stump called Napoleon's Elbow, then quit the swamp. Winding his way through the deserted grounds of the Mossland Mansion, he held with tradition and threw part of his catch to the waterfowl that lived in the old garden pool. Since slavery times, fishermen believed that feeding these birds would bring them luck the next time out.

Thief! Thief! A fish crow spied Hugh Thomas's catch and sent up a signal. Birds darkened the sky. They swooped down, speared their fish, and soared away, screeching, *Thief! Thief!*

"Shoo!" shouted Hugh Thomas. But the birds chased him across the parish road and under the trestle, stopping just short of the first house in Free Jack's Quarters.

Chantilly, the neighbor girl's cat, was sunning on the porch steps. Her gray eyes were fixed on the wagonful of plump fish.

"Why, it's a Christmas gift!" the cat shouted, excitement swelling her words. "...To see you, that is," she added in a soft purr.

Hugh Thomas was surprised that the cat was talking, and to him. Most of the time, Chantilly wouldn't even look in his direction.

"It's not my custom to report on my mistress's whereabouts. But if you want to see Miss Challie Pearl, she's with Walter Edward, out back in the okra patch. Can't you hear them laughing together?"

Without thinking, Hugh Thomas hopped the fence and disappeared around the house.

Sometime later, he came back with his friend in tow. He was talking all excited and explaining. "Come see for yo'self. It was a million fish!"

Challie Pearl stopped. "What million? I see three little fish."

Hugh Thomas was completely confused. Then he looked at Chantilly and understood. "You tricked me," he accused her. "You ate my fish! Say you did!"

The cat blinked innocently and cleaned her whiskers. Challie Pearl scooped up her pet. "You must be addled, Hugh Thomas! Come tellin' that whopper, then layin' blame on my poor, precious kitty-cat." And she marched away in a huff.

Meanwhile a chorus of Chantilly's friends meowed contentedly as they licked their paws.

With only three fish left, Hugh Thomas followed the path to the backwater slough where Papa-Daddy and Elder Abbajon's houseboat was tied up. They were sitting on the front porch playing checkers.

"Seems the bayou let you come 'way with a fine catch this morning," Elder Abbajon said, smiling.

"Best luck a fisherman can have is to catch just enough for dinner," Papa-Daddy put in.

"But I caught a million more," the boy boasted. "What happened to 'em is a long story."

Papa-Daddy pulled his straw hat down over his eyes. Elder Abbajon leaned back in the old cane chair. And both of them propped their feet up on the railing. "So, you've learned that the Bayou Clapateaux is a mighty strange place."

"Tell us, now, was it *really* a million?"

A smile broke across Hugh Thomas's face, and he winked his eye. "More or less," he answered, and started right in on his tale.

A Boy, a Dog and a Frog

Written and illustrated by Mercer Mayer

Originally published in 1967

This is one of the first—and best—stories told without words. The pictures, in their storyboard arrangement, encourage children to tell the story as they see it by creating their own dialogue and narration.

MILLIONS OF CATS

Written and illustrated by Wanda Gág

Originally published in 1928

Once upon a time there was a very old man and a very old woman. They lived in a nice clean house which had flowers all around it, except where the door was. But they couldn't be happy because they were so very lonely.

"If we only had a cat!" sighed the very old woman.

"A cat?" asked the very old man.

"Yes, a sweet little fluffy cat," said the very old woman.

"I will get you a cat, my dear," said the very old man.

And he set out over the hills to look for one. He climbed over the sunny hills. He trudged through the cool valleys. He walked a long, long time and at last he came to a hill which was quite covered with cats.

Cats here, cats there,
Cats and kittens everywhere,
Hundreds of cats,
Thousands of cats,
Millions and billions and trillions of cats.

"Oh," cried the old man joyfully, "now I can choose the prettiest cat and take it home with me!" So he chose one. It was white.

But just as he was about to leave, he saw another one all black and white and it seemed just as pretty as the first. So he took this one also.

But then he saw a fuzzy grey kitten way over here which was every bit as pretty as the others so he took it too.

And now he saw one way down in a corner which he thought too lovely to leave so he took this too.

And just then, over here, the very old man found a kitten which was black and very beautiful.

"It would be a shame to leave that one," said the very old man. So he took it.

And now, over there, he saw a cat which had brown and yellow stripes like a baby tiger.

"I simply must take it!" cried the very old man, and he did.

So it happened that every time the very old man looked up, he saw another cat which was so

pretty he could not bear to leave it, and before he knew it, he had chosen them all.

And so he went back over the sunny hills and down through the cool valleys, to show all his pretty kittens to the very old woman.

It was very funny to see those hundreds and thousands and millions and billions and trillions of cats following him.

They came to a pond.

"Mew, mew! We are thirsty!" cried the
                    Hundreds of cats,
                    Thousands of cats,
Millions and billions and trillions of cats.

"Well, here is a great deal of water," said the very old man.

Each cat took a sip of water, and the pond was gone!

"Mew, mew! Now we are hungry!" said the
                    Hundreds of cats,
                    Thousands of cats,
Millions and billions and trillions of cats.

"There is much grass on the hills," said the very old man.

Each cat ate a mouthful of grass and not a blade was left!

Pretty soon the very old woman saw them coming.

"My dear!" she cried, "What are you doing? I asked for one little cat, and what do I see?—
                "Cats here, cats there,
            Cats and kittens everywhere,
                    Hundreds of cats,
                    Thousands of cats,
Millions and billions and trillions of cats.

"But we can never feed them all," said the very old woman. "They will eat us out of house and home."

"I never thought of that," said the very old man. "What shall we do?"

The very old woman thought for a while and then she said, "I know! We will let the cats decide which one we should keep."

"Oh yes," said the very old man, and he called to the cats, "Which one of you is the prettiest?"

"I am!"

"I am!"

"No, I am!"

"No, I am the prettiest!" "I am!"

"No, I am! I am! I am!" cried hundreds and thousands and millions and billions and trillions of voices, for each cat thought itself the prettiest.

And they began to quarrel.

They bit and scratched and clawed each other and made such a great noise that the very old man and the very old woman ran into the house as fast as they could. They did not like such quarreling. But after a while the noise stopped and the very old man and the very old woman peeped out of the window to see what had happened. They could not see a single cat!

"I think they must have eaten each other all up," said the very old woman. "It's too bad!"

"But look!" said the very old man, and he pointed to a bunch of high grass. In it sat one little frightened kitten. They went out and picked it up. It was thin and scraggly.

"Poor little kitty," said the very old woman.

"Dear little kitty," said the very old man, "how does it happen that you were not eaten up with all those hundreds and thousands and millions and billions and trillions of cats?"

"Oh, I'm just a very homely little cat," said the kitten. "So when you asked who was the prettiest, I didn't say anything. So nobody bothered about me."

They took the kitten into the house, where the very old woman gave it a warm bath and brushed its fur until it was soft and shiny.

Every day they gave it plenty of milk—and soon it grew nice and plump.

"And it is a very pretty cat, after all!" said the very old woman.

"It is the most beautiful cat in the whole world," said the very old man. "I ought to know, for I've seen—

Hundreds of cats,
Thousands of cats,
Millions and billions and trillions of cats—
and not one was as pretty as this one."

GUESS HOW MUCH I LOVE YOU

Written by Sam McBratney
Illustrated by Anita Jeram

Originally published in 1994

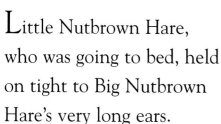
Little Nutbrown Hare,
who was going to bed, held
on tight to Big Nutbrown
Hare's very long ears.

He wanted to be sure that Big
Nutbrown Hare was listening.
"Guess how much I love you,"
he said.

"Oh, I don't think I could guess
that," said Big Nutbrown Hare.

"This much," said Little Nutbrown Hare, stretching out his arms as wide as they could go.

Big Nutbrown Hare had even longer arms. "But I love *you* this much," he said.

Hmm, that is a lot, thought Little Nutbrown Hare.

"I love you as high as
I can reach," said Little
Nutbrown Hare.

"I love you
as high as
I can reach,"
said Big
Nutbrown
Hare.

That is very
high, thought
Little Nutbrown
Hare. I wish
I had arms
like that.

Then Little
Nutbrown Hare
had a good idea.
He tumbled
upside down
and reached
up the tree
trunk with
his feet.

"I love you
all the way up
to my toes!"
he said.

"And *I* love you all
the way up
to your toes," said
Big Nutbrown Hare,
swinging him up
over his head.

"I love you
    as high as
I can hop!"
    laughed Little
        Nutbrown Hare,

bouncing up
    and down.

"But I love you as high as
I can hop," smiled Big
Nutbrown Hare—and he
hopped so high that his ears
touched the branches above.

That's good
hopping,
thought
Little
Nutbrown
Hare.
I wish I
could hop
like that.

"I love you all the way down the lane as far as the river," cried Little Nutbrown Hare.

"I love you across the river and over the hills," said Big Nutbrown Hare.

That's very far, thought Little Nutbrown Hare. He was almost too sleepy to think anymore.

Then he looked beyond the thornbushes, out into the big dark night. Nothing could be farther than the sky.

"I love you right up to the moon," he said, and closed his eyes.

"Oh, that's far," said Big Nutbrown Hare. "That is very, very far."

Big Nutbrown Hare settled Little Nutbrown Hare into his bed of leaves.

He leaned over and kissed him good night.

Then he lay down close by and whispered with a smile, "I love you right up to the moon — and back."

ALEXANDER AND THE TERRIBLE, HORRIBLE, NO GOOD, VERY BAD DAY

Written by Judith Viorst
Illustrated by Ray Cruz

Originally published in 1972

I went to sleep with gum in my mouth and now there's gum in my hair and when I got out of bed this morning I tripped on the skateboard and by mistake I dropped my sweater in the sink while the water was running and I could tell it was going to be a terrible, horrible, no good, very bad day.

At breakfast Anthony found a Corvette Sting Ray car kit in his breakfast cereal box and Nick found a Junior Undercover Agent code ring in his breakfast cereal box but in my breakfast cereal box all I found was breakfast cereal.

I think I'll move to Australia.

In the car pool Mrs. Gibson let Becky have a seat by the window. Audrey and Elliott got seats by the window too. I said I was being scrunched. I said I was being smushed. I said, if I don't get a seat by the window I am going to be carsick. No one even answered.

I could tell it was going to be a terrible, horrible, no good, very bad day.

At school Mrs. Dickens liked Paul's picture of the sailboat better than my picture of the invisible castle.

At singing time she said I sang too loud.

At counting time she said I left out sixteen. Who needs sixteen?

I could tell it was going to be a terrible, horrible, no good, very bad day.

I could tell because Paul said I wasn't his best friend anymore. He said that Philip Parker was his best friend and that Albert Moyo was his next best friend and that I was only his third best friend.

I hope you sit on a tack, I said to Paul. I hope the next time you get a double-decker strawberry ice-cream cone the ice cream part falls off the cone part and lands in Australia.

There were two cupcakes in Philip Parker's lunch bag and Albert got a Hershey bar with almonds and Paul's mother gave him a piece of jelly roll that had little coconut sprinkles on the top. Guess whose mother forgot to put in dessert?

It was a terrible, horrible, no good, very bad day.

That's what it was, because after school my mom took us all to the dentist and Dr. Fields found a cavity just in me. Come back next week and I'll fix it, said Dr. Fields.

Next week, I said, I'm going to Australia.

On the way downstairs the elevator door closed on my foot and while we were waiting for my mom to go get the car Anthony made me fall where it was muddy and then when I started crying because of the mud Nick said I was a crybaby and while I was punching Nick for saying crybaby my mom came back with the car and scolded me for being muddy and fighting.

I am having a terrible, horrible, no good, very bad day, I told everybody. No one even answered.

So then we went to the shoestore to buy some sneakers. Anthony chose white ones with blue stripes. Nick chose red ones with white stripes. I chose blue ones with red stripes but then the shoe man said, We're all sold out. They made me buy plain old white ones, but they can't make me wear them.

When we picked up my dad at his office he said I couldn't play with his copying machine, but I forgot. He also said to watch out for the books on his desk, and I was careful as could be except for my elbow. He also said don't fool around with his phone, but I think I called Australia. My dad said please don't pick him up anymore.

It was a terrible, horrible, no good, very bad day.

There were lima beans for dinner and I hate limas.

There was kissing on TV and I hate kissing.

My bath was too hot, I got soap in my eyes, my marble went down the drain, and I had to wear my railroad-train pajamas. I hate my railroad-train pajamas.

When I went to bed Nick took back the pillow he said I could keep and the Mickey Mouse night light burned out and I bit my tongue.

The cat wants to sleep with Anthony, not with me.

It has been a terrible, horrible, no good, very bad day.

My mom says some days are like that.

Even in Australia.

CURIOUS GEORGE

Written and illustrated by H. A. Rey

Originally published in 1941

This is George.
He lived in Africa.
He was a good little monkey
and always very curious.

One day George saw a man.
He had on a large yellow straw hat.
The man saw George too. "What a nice
little monkey," he thought. "I would like to
take him home with me."

He put his hat on the ground
and, of course, George was curious.
He came down from the tree
to look at the large yellow hat.

The hat had been on the man's head.
George thought it would be nice
to have it on his own head.
He picked it up and put it on.

The hat covered George's head.
He couldn't see.

The man picked him up quickly and
popped him into a bag. George was caught.

The man with the big yellow hat put George into a little boat, and a sailor rowed them both across the water to a big ship. George was sad, but he was still a little curious.

On the big ship, things began to happen. The man took off the bag. George sat on a little stool and the man said, "George, I am going to take you to a big Zoo in a big city. You will like it there. Now run along and play, but don't get into trouble."

George promised to be good. But it is easy for little monkeys to forget.

On the deck he found some sea gulls. He wondered how they could fly. He was very curious. Finally he HAD to try. It looked easy. But— oh, what happened!

First this—

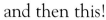

and then this!

"WHERE IS GEORGE?"

The sailors looked and looked. At last they saw him struggling in the water, and almost all tired out.

"Man overboard!" the sailors cried as they threw him a lifebelt. George caught it and held on. At last he was safe on board.

After that George was more careful to be a good monkey, until, at last, the long trip was over.

George said good-bye to the kind sailors, and he and the man with the yellow hat walked off the ship on to the shore and on into the city to the man's house.

After a good meal and a good pipe George felt very tired.

He crawled into bed and fell asleep at once.

The next morning the man telephoned the Zoo. George watched him. He was fascinated. Then the man went away.

George was curious. He wanted to telephone, too. One, two, three, four, five, six, seven. What fun!

DING-A-LING-A-LING! GEORGE HAD TELEPHONED THE FIRE STATION!

The firemen rushed to the telephone. "Hello! Hello!" they said. But there was no answer.

Then they looked for the signal on the big map that showed where the telephone call had come from. They didn't know it was GEORGE. They thought it was a real fire.

HURRY! HURRY! HURRY!

The firemen jumped on to the fire engines and on to the hook-and-ladders. Ding-dong-ding-dong. Everyone out of the way!

Hurry! Hurry! Hurry!

The firemen rushed into the house. They opened the door. NO FIRE! ONLY a naughty little monkey.

"Oh, catch him, catch him," they cried. George tried to run away. He almost did, but he got caught in the telephone wire, and—a thin fireman caught one arm and a fat fireman caught the other.

"You fooled the fire department," they said. "We will have to shut you up where you can't do any more harm."

They took him away and shut him in a prison.

George wanted to get out. He climbed up to the window to try the bars.

Just then the watchman came in. He got on the wooden bed to catch George. But he was too big and heavy.

The bed tipped up, the watchman fell over, and, quick as lightning, George ran out through the open door.

He hurried through the building and out on to the roof. And then he was lucky to be a monkey: out he walked on to the telephone wires. Quickly and quietly over the guard's head, George walked away.

He was free!

Down in the street outside the prison wall stood a balloon man. A little girl bought a balloon for her brother.

George watched. He was curious again. He felt he MUST have a bright red balloon. He reached over and tried to help himself, but—instead of one balloon, the whole bunch broke loose.

In an instant the wind whisked them all away and, with them, went George, holding tight with both hands.

Up, up he sailed, higher and higher. The houses looked like toy houses and the people like dolls. George was frightened. He held on very tight.

At first the wind blew in great gusts. Then it quieted.

Finally it stopped blowing altogether. George was very tired. Down, down he went—bump, on to the top of a traffic light.

Everyone was surprised. The traffic got all mixed up. George didn't know what to do, and then he heard someone call, "GEORGE!"

He looked down and saw his friend, the man with the big yellow hat!

George was very happy. The man was happy too. George slid down the post and the man with the big yellow hat put him under his arm.

Then he paid the balloon man for all the balloons.

And then George and the man climbed into the car and at last away they went to the ZOO!

What a nice place for George to live!

I HEAR, I SEE, I TOUCH

Written and illustrated by Helen Oxenbury

Originally published in 1985

I HEAR

bird

rain

dog

watch

telephone

baby

I See

butterfly

frog

airplane

friend

flower

moon

I TOUCH

ball

beard

worm

cat

water

blanket

MISS NELSON IS MISSING!

Written by Harry Allard
Illustrated by James Marshall

Originally published in 1977

The kids in Room 207 were misbehaving again.

Spitballs stuck to the ceiling.

Paper planes whizzed through the air.

They were the worst-behaved class in the whole school.

"Now settle down," said Miss Nelson in a sweet voice.

But the class would *not* settle down.

They whispered and giggled.

They squirmed and made faces.

They were even rude during story hour.

And they always refused to do their lessons.

"Something will have to be done," said Miss Nelson.

The next morning Miss Nelson did not come to school.

"Wow!" yelled the kids. "Now we can *really* act up!"

They began to make more spitballs and paper planes.

"Today let's be just terrible!" they said.

"Not so fast!" hissed an unpleasant voice.

A woman in an ugly black dress stood before them.

"I am your new teacher, Miss Viola Swamp."

And she rapped the desk with her ruler.

"Where is Miss Nelson?" asked the kids.

"Never mind that!" snapped Miss Swamp. "Open those arithmetic books!"

Miss Nelson's kids did as they were told.

They could see that Miss Swamp was a real witch.

She meant business.

Right away she put them to work.

And she loaded them down with homework.

"We'll have no story hour today," said Miss Swamp.

"Keep your mouths shut," said Miss Swamp.

"Sit perfectly still," said Miss Swamp.

"And if you misbehave, you'll be sorry," said Miss Swamp.

The kids in Room 207 had *never* worked so hard.

Days went by and there was no sign of Miss Nelson.

The kids *missed* Miss Nelson!

"Maybe we should try to find her," they said.

Some of them went to the police.

Detective McSmogg was assigned to the case.

He listened to their story.

He scratched his chin.

"Hmmmm," he said. "Hmmm."

"I think Miss Nelson is missing."

Detective McSmogg would not be much help.

Other kids went to Miss Nelson's house.

The shades were tightly drawn, and no one answered the door.

In fact, the only person they *did* see was the wicked Miss Viola Swamp, coming up the street.

"If she sees us, she'll give us more homework."

They got away just in time.

Maybe something *terrible* happened to Miss Nelson!

"Maybe she was gobbled up by a shark!" said one of the kids.

But that didn't seem likely.

"Maybe Miss Nelson went to Mars!" said another kid.

But that didn't seem likely either.

"I know!" exclaimed one know-it-all. "Maybe Miss Nelson's car was carried off by a swarm of angry butterflies!"

But that was the least likely of all.

The kids in Room 207 became very discouraged. It seemed that Miss Nelson was never coming back. And they would be stuck with Miss Viola Swamp forever.

They heard footsteps in the hall.

"Here comes the witch," they whispered.

"Hello, children," someone said in a sweet voice.

It was Miss Nelson!

"Did you miss me?" she asked.

"We certainly did!" cried all the kids.

"Where were you?"

"That's my little secret," said Miss Nelson.

"How about a story hour?"

"Oh yes!" cried the kids.

Miss Nelson noticed that during story hour no one was rude or silly.

"What brought about this lovely change?" she asked.

"That's *our* little secret," said the kids.

Back home Miss Nelson took off her coat and hung it in the closet (right next to an ugly black dress).

When it was time for bed she sang a little song. "I'll never tell," she said to herself with a smile.

P.S. Detective McSmogg is working on a new case.

He is *now* looking for Miss Viola Swamp.

TITCH

Written and illustrated by Pat Hutchins

Originally published in 1971

Titch was little.

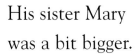

His sister Mary
was a bit bigger.

And his brother Pete
was a lot bigger.

Pete had a great big bike.

Mary had a big bike.

And Titch had a little tricycle.

Pete had a kite
that flew high
above the trees.

Mary had a kite
that flew high
above the houses.

And Titch had a pinwheel
that he held in his hand.

Pete had a big drum.

Mary had a trumpet.

And Titch had
a little wooden whistle.

Pete had a big saw.

Mary had a big hammer.

And Titch held
the nails.

Pete had a big spade.

Mary had a fat flowerpot.

But Titch had
the tiny seed.

And Titch's seed grew

and grew

and grew.

WHERE THE WILD THINGS ARE

Story and pictures by Maurice Sendak

Originally published in 1963

The night Max wore his wolf suit
and made mischief of one kind

and another

his mother called him "WILD THING!"

and Max said "I'LL EAT YOU UP!"

so he was sent to bed without eating anything.

That very night in Max's room a forest grew

and grew—

and grew until his ceiling hung with vines
and the walls became the world all around

and an ocean tumbled by with a private boat for Max
and he sailed off through night and day

and in and out of weeks
and almost over a year
to where the wild things are.

And when he came to the place where the wild things are
they roared their terrible roars and gnashed their terrible teeth

till Max said "BE STILL!"
and tamed them with the magic trick

and rolled their terrible eyes and showed their terrible claws

of staring into all their yellow eyes without blinking once
and they were frightened and called him the most wild thing of all

and made him king of all wild things.

"And now," cried Max, "let the wild rumpus start!"

"Now stop!" Max said and sent the wild things off to bed
without their supper. And Max the king of all wild things was lonely
and wanted to be where someone loved him best of all.

But the wild things cried, "Oh please don't go—
we'll eat you up—we love you so!"
And Max said, "No!"

Then all around from far away across the world
he smelled good things to eat
so he gave up being king of where the wild things are.

he wild things roared their terrible roars and gnashed their terrible teeth
nd rolled their terrible eyes and showed their terrible claws
ut Max stepped into his private boat and waved good-bye

and sailed back over a year
and in and out of weeks
and through a day

and into the night of his very own room
where he found his supper waiting for him

and it was still hot.

THE CAT CLUB

Written and illustrated by Esther Averill

Originally published in 1944

In Captain Tinker's garden, once upon a time, there was a Cat Club. All the cats and kittens in the neighborhood were members. All but Jenny Linsky.

Jenny Linsky was a small black orphan cat who lived with Captain Tinker.

He had found Jenny in the street where a dog was chasing her. No one knew where she had come from and the Captain took her home.

He was very kind to Jenny. She had cream and chicken every night for supper. Her coal black fur grew soft and glossy. Her yellow eyes began to have a happy look.

One day the Captain said to her, "You and I must always be best friends."

That made Jenny's heart beat fast.

But the Captain added gently, "I think a little cat like you should go outdoors sometimes and play. Lots of nice cats live in this garden."

Jenny had often heard the Cat Club singing after dark.

"They do have fun," she thought.

But she was too shy to say "hello" to them.

"Shy little cats need help," thought Captain Tinker to himself.

Captain Tinker, who was an old sailor, liked to make things and many years ago had learned to knit. He knitted a woolen scarf for Jenny—a bright red woolen scarf to go with her black fur and yellow eyes.

How Jenny loved that scarf! How brave she felt when she was wearing it! And one fine night she put it on and went into the garden.

It was a lovely garden full of flowers and trees and bushes. On three sides were rows of pink brick houses. On the other side was a tall board fence that kept the dogs away. Jenny and the Captain lived in the brick house that was covered with ivy.

Jenny crept softly through the grass and found a hiding place beneath a rosebush. There she waited for the Cat Club. She waited a long time.

Suddenly a slim white cat sped through the grass, dashed up the maple tree and began to sing. This was Concertina, the Club Secretary. She sang:

Come all ye cats and kittens
With your whiskers and your mittens
Come a-running, come a-running
To the Cat Club Jamboree.

Mr. President came first.

Mr. President was a well-fed cat who always wore a collar with his name and number on a tag. He walked slowly out of his brick house and took his place—the "Chair," he called it— on the meeting ground beneath the maple tree.

Then the others came. They came one by one and two by two from darkened doorways and over the tall board fence. They formed a circle in front of Mr. President.

CONCERTINA, IN THE MAPLE TREE, GIVES
THE SIGNAL FOR THE CATS TO COME

Just before the meeting, MR. PRESIDENT speaks to his young nephew, JUNIOR. The fluffy cat is BUTTERFLY. The twins are ROMULUS and REMUS. The cat jumping over a flower is MACARONI. SOLOMON, the wise cat who can read, sits on his books and watches the two great fighters, SINBAD and THE DUKE. The two cats in earnest conversation are the sweethearts, ARABELLA and ANTONIO.

Mr. President opened the meeting and spoke a few brief words about a money matter. Afterwards the Club moved to the porch of Concertina's house.

Jenny stretched her neck and peeping through the rose leaves saw everything that happened.

The spotted twin cats, Romulus and Remus, crawled through the kitchen window and returned with a large paper package.

"A feast! A fish!" cried all the cats.

They tore off the paper and devoured the fish.

After they had licked their paws and whiskers, the lovely Persian cat, Butterfly, brought out her nose flute and began to play. The cats sang and danced and joked until the wee small hours when, one by one, the Club went home.

The last cat to go was Jenny Linsky. She had not dreamed that cats could have such fun.

Night after night she crept into the garden and watched the Cat Club from behind the rosebush.

"What clever cats they are!" sighed Jenny. "All of them can do things. Look at Butterfly. She plays a nose flute. Look at Macaroni. He can dance on his hind legs. And what can I do?"

Poor little Jenny! There was nothing she could do. But she was content to watch the others at their fun and frolic.

One night, to her surprise, Romulus and Remus, who were going to the meeting, poked their noses right into the rosebush and cried gaily, "Hi there, sister, you're the new cat, aren't you?"

The twins were in such lively spirits that Jenny did not feel afraid.

"Yes," she answered, "I am Jenny Linsky."

"Well, Jenny, wouldn't you like to join the Cat Club?" asked the twins.

They did not give her time to answer. They whisked her off between them.

But when they reached the meeting ground, fear overcame her. All the other cats were there, staring at her with their gleaming eyes, as if to say, "And what can you do, little black cat? WHAT CAN YOU DO?"

This was too much for Jenny. She gave a yowl of terror and fled home.

Next morning Romulus and Remus went to Jenny's house, looked through the garden window and called, "Jenny! Jenny Linsky!"

Jenny did not answer. She was lying on a soapbox in the cellar.

The twins had come to cheer her up and they went away, discouraged.

In the afternoon the Persian cat, the lovely one named Butterfly, pressed her silky face against the windowpane and called, "Jenny! Jenny Linsky!"

Jenny Linsky did not answer. She was still lying on the soapbox in the cellar.

Butterfly, too, went off, discouraged.

In the evening the entire Cat Club, singing loudly, trooped through the garden on their way to Jenny's house.

Mr. President came first.

Behind him walked Butterfly, playing on her nose flute.

Concertina followed. She had a high soprano voice and led the singing, and behind her, one by one or two by two, the singers marched.

First came Romulus and Remus.

Next, Mr. President's young nephew, Junior, accompanied by Solomon, the bookish cat.

The fancy dancer, Macaroni, followed. He was waltzing.

Behind Macaroni came the sweethearts, Arabella and Antonio.

Lastly marched the two great fighters, Sinbad and the Duke.

All of them were singing:

> Meow and a purr! We want *her!*
> Jenny! Jenny! Jenny!

Alas! They sang too loudly.

A man who could not sleep threw down a bucketful of water and broke up their fine parade. The members scampered home to dry their dripping fur.

They did not meet again until the following night, when they had other plans and did not go to Jenny's house. It was summer and in the summer Cat Clubs are very busy.

So in the end the Club in Captain Tinker's garden quite forgot poor Jenny Linsky. Still, you cannot blame them. You cannot expect other cats to think always of your troubles.

Jenny who was ashamed of having run away, now stayed indoors. Time dragged. Now and then she played games with Captain Tinker. But when night came and she heard the cats in the garden, she longed to be with them.

"And that will never happen," she sighed. "They are too clever. All of them can do things. What can I do? Nothing."

Time passed.

The birds flew south. The honeysuckle and the rosebush lost their leaves.

Winter came and everything was frozen. Then Captain Tinker flooded the garden and made a pond where the boys and girls could skate.

One day while Jenny watched the skating from the window, she turned suddenly to Captain Tinker.

"I should love to skate," she said. "That's something I *could* do."

Jenny was surprised that Captain Tinker did not answer. She went to him and put her paw upon his arm.

"Captain," she said, "if I could only have some skates."

Captain Tinker remained silent. He sat in his armchair, puffing at his pipe and looking thoughtful. Jenny did not know that out of the corner of his eye the Captain watched her as she climbed the stairs.

Upstairs she hunted for skates in bureau drawers and on the closet shelves. She found nothing.

In the night while Captain Tinker was asleep, Jenny came downstairs and searched the downstairs closets.

She ransacked the drawer where Captain Tinker kept his fishing tackle. She found hooks and lines and corks—but no skates.

In November it snowed—the first snow storm Jenny had ever seen. All afternoon she watched the snowflakes falling.

By evening the garden was entirely white. Jenny stole outdoors and hunted in the drifts. She found snowflakes shaped like flowers and stars and spiderwebs—but no skates.

"I'm glad Jenny has gone outdoors at last," thought Captain Tinker. "Now we shall see what we shall see."

Bright and early the following day the Captain went to his workshop in the cellar. He closed the door behind him and would not let Jenny in. All morning she could hear him tapping with his hammer.

The mysterious hammering and tapping went on for many days. On Christmas Eve Captain Tinker came upstairs with something in his pocket. Jenny watched him as he lit the Christmas candle and pulled back the curtain.

"The stars are out," said Captain Tinker, looking at the sky.

As he said it, he took out of his pocket four little—

Could they be real?

Jenny stared.

She reached out and touched them—oh, so gently—with her paw. They were real, and they were silver, and they had sharp shiny blades.

"Ice skates!" she whispered. "Silver ice skates! Oh, Captain . . ."

The Captain strapped the skates on Jenny's paws. They fitted exactly. Her ankles wobbled for a moment; then she felt quite steady. Captain Tinker tied her scarf and she went into the garden.

At the pond she hesitated.

"Which paw goes first?" she wondered.

She struck forth on her right front paw and glided. Then with her left hind paw she gave a shove and glided further. She began to skim across the ice.

It was a pretty sight to see her skating with her red muffler streaming, and her bright skates flashing in the moonlight. She cut figure eights and flowers and stars.

The Cat Club saw her. They were at the other end of the pond and had been singing Christmas carols. Their mouths hung open and their bulging eyes were fixed on Jenny Linsky.

No one in the Club had ever seen a cat skate.

Suddenly Romulus and Remus cried, "Jenny! Jenny Linsky!"

And all the other cats cried, "Jenny! Jenny Linsky!"

She glided toward them.

Romulus and Remus dashed to meet her and before she knew it she was standing in front of Mr. President.

"Mr. President," said Romulus and Remus, "we hope that this black cat, a friend of ours, will now be asked to join the Club."

Mr. President looked at Jenny with his beady eyes.

"What is your name?" he asked.

"Jenny Linsky," she replied.

"Where do you live?"

"In Captain Tinker's house."

"Can you do anything?" asked Mr. President.

"I can skate," said Jenny proudly.

"Yippetty-yip-yip-yip!" cried all the cats.

When the cheering died down, Mr. President addressed the Club, saying, "The question is, Shall our distinguished guest, Miss Jenny Linsky, who can skate, be asked to join the Cat Club? All cats in favor raise a right front paw."

Every member raised a right front paw.

"All cats opposed kick a left hind leg."

No one kicked a left hind leg.

Two cats went into the bushes to count the votes. They came back quickly and whispered in Mr. President's ear. Mr. President looked satisfied.

He turned to Jenny.

"Miss Jenny Linsky," said Mr. President, "the votes have been counted. I have the noble honor to inform you that you are a member of the Cat Club."

"Mr. President," said Jenny in a high clear voice, "and you, my trusty friends, I thank you."

Jenny could have made a longer speech. But the Cat Club crowded around her, hoping for a chance to touch the silver skates.

SYLVESTER AND THE MAGIC PEBBLE

Written and illustrated by William Steig

Originally published in 1969

Sylvester Duncan lived with his mother and father at Acorn Road in Oatsdale. One of his hobbies was collecting pebbles of unusual shape and color.

On a rainy Saturday during vacation he found a quite extraordinary one. It was flaming red, shiny, and perfectly round, like a marble. As he was studying this remarkable pebble, he began to shiver, probably from excitement, and the rain felt cold on his back. "I wish it would stop raining," he said.

To his great surprise the rain stopped. It didn't stop gradually as rains usually do. It CEASED. The drops vanished on the way down, the clouds disappeared, everything was dry, and the sun was shining as if rain had never existed.

In all his young life Sylvester had never had a wish gratified so quickly. It struck him that magic must be at work, and he guessed that the magic must be in the remarkable-looking red pebble. (Where indeed it was.) To make a test, he put the pebble on the ground and said, "I wish it would rain again." Nothing happened. But when he said the same thing holding the pebble in his hoof, the sky turned black, there was lightning and a clap of thunder, and the rain came shooting down.

"What a lucky day this is!" thought Sylvester. "From now on I can have anything I want. My father and mother can have anything they want. My relatives, my friends, and anybody at all can have everything anybody wants!"

He wished the sunshine back in the sky, and he wished a wart on his left hind fetlock would disappear, and it did, and he started home, eager to amaze his father and mother with his magic pebble. He could hardly wait to see their faces. Maybe they wouldn't even believe him at first.

126

As he was crossing Strawberry Hill, thinking of some of the many, many things he could wish for, he was startled to see a mean, hungry lion looking right at him from behind some tall grass. He was frightened. If he hadn't been so frightened, he could have made the lion disappear, or he could have wished himself safe at home with his father and mother.

He could have wished the lion would turn into a butterfly or a daisy or a gnat. He could have wished many things, but he panicked and couldn't think carefully.

"I wish I were a rock," he said, and he became a rock.

The lion came bounding over, sniffed the rock a hundred times, walked around and around it, and went away confused, perplexed, puzzled, and bewildered. "I saw that little donkey as clear as day. Maybe I'm going crazy," he muttered.

And there was Sylvester, a rock on Strawberry Hill, with the magic pebble lying right beside him on the ground, and he was unable to pick it up. "Oh, how I wish I were myself again," he thought, but nothing happened. He had to be touching the pebble to make the magic work, but there was nothing he could do about it.

His thoughts began to race like mad. He was scared and worried. Being helpless, he felt hopeless. He imagined all the possibilities, and eventually he realized that his only chance of becoming himself again was for someone to find the red pebble and to wish that the rock next to it would be a donkey. Someone would surely find the red pebble—it was so bright and shiny—but what on earth would make them wish that a rock were a donkey? The chance was one in a billion at best.

Sylvester fell asleep. What else could he do? Night came with many stars.

Meanwhile, back at home, Mr. and Mrs. Duncan paced the floor, frantic with worry. Sylvester had never come home later than dinner time. Where could he be? They stayed up all night wondering what had happened, expecting that Sylvester would surely turn up by morning. But he didn't, of course. Mrs. Duncan cried a lot and Mr. Duncan did his best to soothe her. Both longed to have their dear son with them.

"I will never scold Sylvester again as long as I live," said Mrs. Duncan, "no matter what he does."

At dawn, they went about inquiring of all the neighbors.

They talked to all the children—the puppies, the kittens, the colts, the piglets. No one had seen Sylvester since the day before yesterday.

They went to the police. The police could not find their child.

All the dogs in Oatsdale went searching for him. They sniffed behind every rock and tree and blade of grass, into every nook and gully of the neighborhood and beyond, but found not a scent of him. They sniffed the rock on Strawberry Hill, but it smelled like a rock. It didn't smell like Sylvester.

After a month of searching the same places over and over again, and inquiring of the same animals over and over again, Mr. and Mrs. Duncan no longer knew what to do. They concluded that something dreadful must have happened and that they would probably never see their son again. (Though all the time he was less than a mile away.)

They tried their best to be happy, to go about their usual ways. But their usual ways included Sylvester and they were always reminded of him. They were miserable. Life had no meaning for them any more.

Night followed day and day followed night over and over again. Sylvester on the hill woke up less and less often. When he was awake, he was only hopeless and unhappy. He felt he would be a rock forever and he tried to get used to it. He went into an endless sleep. The days grew colder. Fall came with the leaves changing color. Then the leaves fell and the grass bent to the ground.

Then it was winter. The winds blew, this way and that. It snowed. Mostly, the animals stayed indoors, living on the food they had stored up.

One day a wolf sat on the rock that was Sylvester and howled and howled because he was hungry.

Then the snows melted. The earth warmed up in the spring sun and things budded.

Leaves were on the trees again. Flowers showed their young faces.

One day in May, Mr. Duncan insisted that his wife go with him on a picnic. "Let's cheer up," he said. "Let us try to live again and be happy even though Sylvester, our angel, is no longer with us." They went to Strawberry Hill.

Mrs. Duncan sat down on the rock. The warmth of his own mother sitting on him woke Sylvester up from his deep winter sleep. How he wanted to shout, "Mother! Father! It's me, Sylvester, I'm right here!" But he couldn't talk. He had no voice. He was stone-dumb.

Mr. Duncan walked aimlessly about while Mrs. Duncan set out the picnic food on the rock—alfalfa sandwiches, pickled oats, sassafras salad, timothy compote. Suddenly Mr. Duncan saw the red pebble. "What a fantastic pebble!" he exclaimed. "Sylvester would have loved it for his collection." He put the pebble on the rock.

They sat down to eat. Sylvester was now as wide awake as a donkey that was a rock could possibly be. Mrs. Duncan felt some mysterious excitement. "You know, Father," she said suddenly, "I have the strangest feeling that our dear Sylvester is still alive and not far away."

"I am, I am!" Sylvester wanted to shout, but he couldn't. If only he had realized that the pebble resting on his back was the magic pebble!

"Oh, how I wish he were here with us on this lovely May day," said Mrs. Duncan. Mr. Duncan looked sadly at the ground. "Don't you wish it too, Father?" she said. He looked at her as if to say, "How can you ask such a question?"

Mr. and Mrs. Duncan looked at each other with great sorrow.

"I wish I were myself again, I wish I were my real self again!" thought Sylvester.

And in that instant, he was!

You can imagine the scene that followed—the embraces, the kisses, the questions, the answers, the loving looks, and the fond exclamations!

When they had eventually calmed down a bit, and had gotten home, Mr. Duncan put the magic pebble in an iron safe. Some day they might want to use it, but really, for now, what more could they wish for? They all had all that they wanted.

GOOD NIGHT, GORILLA

Written and illustrated by Peggy Rathmann

Originally published in 1994

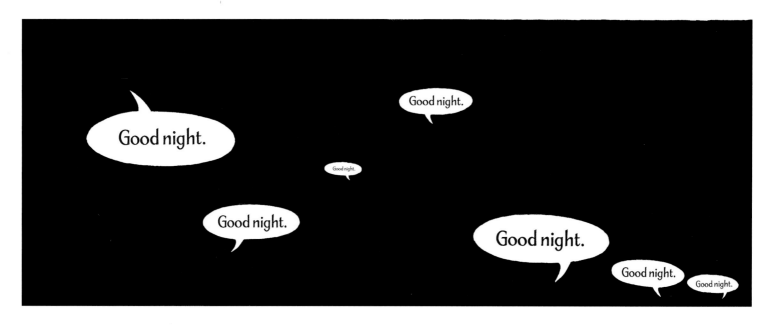

MIKE MULLIGAN AND HIS STEAM SHOVEL

Written and illustrated by Virginia Lee Burton

Originally published in 1939

Mike Mulligan had a steam shovel, a beautiful red steam shovel. Her name was Mary Anne. Mike Mulligan was very proud of Mary Anne. He always said that she could dig as much in a day as a hundred men could dig in a week, but he had never been quite sure that this was true.

Mike Mulligan and Mary Anne had been digging together for years and years. Mike Mulligan took such good care of Mary Anne she never grew old.

It was Mike Mulligan and Mary Anne and some others who dug the great canals for the big boats to sail through.

It was Mike Mulligan and Mary Anne and some others who cut through the high mountains so that trains could go through.

It was Mike Mulligan and Mary Anne and some others who lowered the hills and straightened the curves to make the long highways for the automobiles.

It was Mike Mulligan and Mary Anne and some others who smoothed out the ground and filled in the holes to make the landing fields for the airplanes.

And it was Mike Mulligan and Mary Anne and some others who dug the deep holes for the cellars of the tall skyscrapers in the big cities. When people used to stop and watch them, Mike Mulligan and Mary Anne used to dig a little faster and a little better. The more people stopped, the faster and better they dug. Some days they would keep as many as thirty-seven trucks busy taking away the dirt they had dug.

Then along came the new gasoline shovels and the new electric shovels and the new Diesel motor shovels and took all the jobs away from the steam shovels.

Mike Mulligan and Mary Anne were VERY SAD.

All the other steam shovels were being sold for junk, or left out in old gravel pits to rust and fall apart. Mike loved Mary Anne. He couldn't do that to her. He had taken such good care of her that she could still dig as much in a day as a hundred men could dig in a week; at least he thought she could but he wasn't quite sure. Everywhere they went the new gas shovels and the new electric shovels and the new Diesel motor shovels had all the jobs. No one wanted Mike Mulligan and Mary Anne any more.

Then one day Mike read in a newspaper that the town of Popperville was going to build a new town hall. "We are going to dig the cellar of that town hall," said Mike to Mary Anne, and off they started.

They left the canals and the railroads and the highways and the airports and the big cities where no one wanted them any more and went away out in the country. They crawled along slowly up the hills and down the hills till they came to the little town of Popperville.

When they got there they found that the selectmen were just deciding who should dig the cellar for the new town hall. Mike Mulligan spoke to Henry B. Swap, one of the selectmen. "I heard," he said, "that you are going to build a new town hall. Mary Anne and I will dig the cellar for you in just one day."

"What!" said Henry B. Swap. "Dig a cellar in a day! It would take a hundred men at least a week to dig the cellar for our new town hall."

"Sure," said Mike, "but Mary Anne can dig as much in a day as a hundred men can dig in a week." Though he had never been quite sure that this was true. Then he added, "If we can't do it, you won't have to pay."

Henry B. Swap thought that this would be an easy way to get part of the cellar dug for nothing, so he smiled in rather a mean way and gave the job of digging the cellar of the new town hall to Mike Mulligan and Mary Anne.

They started in early the next morning just as the sun was coming up.

Soon a little boy came along. "Do you think you will finish by sundown?" he said to Mike Mulligan.

"Sure," said Mike, "if you stay and watch us. We always work faster and better when someone is watching us."

So the little boy stayed to watch.

Then Mrs. McGillicuddy, Henry B. Swap, and the Town Constable came over to see what was happening, and they stayed to watch. Mike Mulligan and Mary Anne dug a little faster and a little better.

This gave the little boy a good idea. He ran off and told the postman with the morning mail, the telegraph boy on his bicycle, the milkman with his cart and horse, the doctor on his way home, and the farmer and his family coming to town for the day, and they all stopped and stayed to watch.

That made Mike Mulligan and Mary Anne dig a little faster and a little better. They finished the first corner neat and square . . . but the sun was getting higher.

Clang! Clang! Clang! The Fire Department arrived. They had seen the smoke and thought there was a fire. Then the little boy said, "Why don't you stay and watch?" So the Fire Department of Popperville stayed to watch Mike Mulligan and Mary Anne.

When they heard the fire engine, the children in the school across the street couldn't keep their eyes on their lessons. The teacher called a long recess and the whole school came out to watch. That made Mike Mulligan and Mary Anne dig still faster and still better.

They finished the second corner neat and square, but the sun was right up in the top of the sky.

Now the girl who answers the telephone called up the next towns of Bangerville and Bopperville and Kipperville and Kopperville and told them what was happening in Popperville. All the people came over to see if Mike Mulligan and his steam shovel could dig the cellar in just one day.

The more people came, the faster Mike Mulligan and Mary Anne dug. But they would have to hurry. They were only halfway through and the sun was beginning to go down.

They finished the third corner . . . neat and square.

Never had Mike Mulligan and Mary Anne had so many people to watch them; never had they dug so fast and so well; and never had the sun seemed to go down so fast.

"Hurry, Mike Mulligan! Hurry! Hurry!" shouted the little boy. "There's not much more time!" Dirt was flying everywhere, and the smoke and steam were so thick that the people could hardly see anything.

But listen!

BING! BANG! CRASH! SLAM! LOUDER AND LOUDER, FASTER AND FASTER.

Then suddenly it was quiet. Slowly the dirt settled down. The smoke and steam cleared away, and there was the cellar all finished. Four corners . . . neat and square; four walls . . . straight down, and Mike Mulligan and Mary Anne at the bottom, and the sun was just going down behind the hill.

"Hurray!" shouted the people. "Hurray for Mike Mulligan and his steam shovel! They have dug the cellar in just one day."

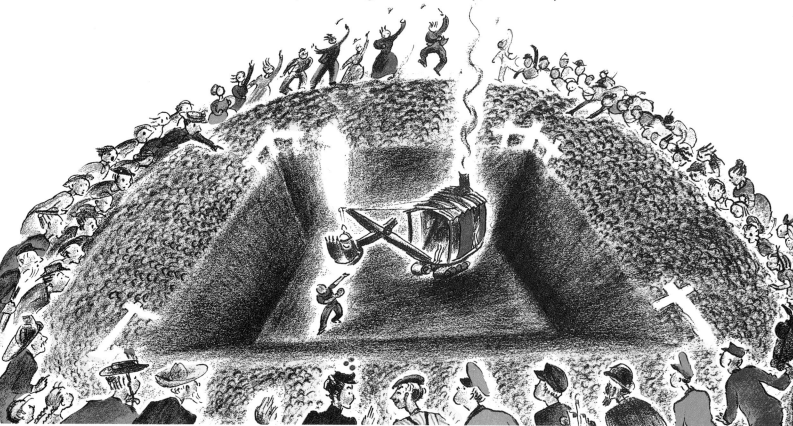

Suddenly the little boy said, "How are they going to get out?"

"That's right," said Mrs. McGillicuddy to Henry B. Swap. "How is he going to get his steam shovel out?"

Henry B. Swap didn't answer, but he smiled in rather a mean way. Then everybody said, "How are they going to get out? Hi! Mike Mulligan! How are you going to get your steam shovel out?"

Mike Mulligan looked around at the four square walls and four square corners, and he said, "We've dug so fast and we've dug so well that we've quite forgotten to leave a way out!" Nothing like this had ever happened to Mike Mulligan and Mary Anne before, and they didn't know what to do.

Nothing like this had ever happened before in Popperville. Everybody started talking at once, and everybody had a different idea, and everybody thought that his idea was the best. They talked and they talked and they argued and they fought till they were worn out, and still no one knew how to get Mike Mulligan and Mary Anne out of the cellar they had dug.

Then Henry B. Swap said, "The job isn't finished because Mary Anne isn't out of the cellar, so Mike Mulligan won't get paid." And he smiled again in a rather mean way.

Now the little boy, who had been keeping very quiet, had another good idea. He said, "Why couldn't we leave Mary Anne in the cellar and build the new town hall above her? Let her be the furnace for the new town hall and let Mike Mulligan be the janitor. Then you wouldn't have to buy a new furnace, and we could pay Mike Mulligan for digging the cellar in just one day."

"Why not?" said Henry B. Swap, and smiled in a way that was not quite so mean.

"Why not?" said Mrs. McGillicuddy.

"Why not?" said the Town Constable.

"Why not?" said all the people.

So they found a ladder and climbed down into the cellar to ask Mike Mulligan and Mary Anne.

"Why not?" said Mike Mulligan. So it was decided, and everybody was happy.

They built the new town hall right over Mike Mulligan and Mary Anne. It was finished before winter.

Every day the little boy goes over to see Mike Mulligan and Mary Anne, and Mrs. McGillicuddy takes him nice hot apple pies. As for Henry B. Swap, he spends most of his time in the cellar of the new town hall listening to the stories that Mike Mulligan has to tell and smiling in a way that isn't mean at all.

Now when you go to Popperville, be sure to go down in the cellar of the new town hall. There they'll be, Mike Mulligan and Mary Anne . . . Mike in his rocking chair smoking his pipe, and Mary Anne beside him, warming up the meetings in the new town hall.

STEVIE

Written and illustrated by John Steptoe

Originally published in 1969

One day my momma told me, "You know you're
gonna have a little friend come stay with you."

And I said, "Who is it?"

And she said, "You know my friend Mrs. Mack? Well,
she has to work all week and I'm gonna keep her little boy."

I asked, "For how long?"

She said, "He'll stay all week and his mother will come
pick him up on Saturdays."

The next day the doorbell rang. It was a lady and a kid. He was smaller than me. I ran to my mother. "Is that them?"

They went in the kitchen but I stayed out in the hall to listen.

The little boy's name was Steven but his mother kept calling him Stevie. My name is Robert but my momma don't call me Robertie.

And so Steve moved in, with his old crybaby self. He always had to have his way. And he was greedy too. Everything he sees he wants.

"Could I have somma that? Gimme this." Man!

Since he was littler than me, while I went to school he used to stay home and play with my toys.

I wished his mother would bring somma *his* toys over here to break up.

I used to get so mad at my mother when I came home after school. "Momma, can't you watch him and tell him to leave my stuff alone?"

Then he used to like to get up on my bed to look out the window and leave his dirty footprints all over my bed. And my momma never said nothin' to him.

And on Saturdays when his mother comes to pick him up, he always tries to act cute just cause his mother is there.

He picked up my airplane and I told him not to bother it. He thought I wouldn't say nothin' to him in front of his mother.

I could never go anywhere without my mother sayin' "Take Stevie with you now."

"But why I gotta take him everywhere I go?" I'd say.

"Now if you were stayin' with someone you wouldn't want them to treat you mean," my mother told me. "Why don't you and Stevie try to play nice?"

Yeah, but I always been nice to him with his old spoiled self. He's always gotta have his way anyway.

I had to take him out to play with me and my friends.

"Is that your brother, Bobby?" they'd ask me.

"No."

"Is that your cousin?"

"No! He's just my friend and he's stayin' at my house and my mother made me bring him."

"Ha, ha. You gotta baby-sit! Bobby the baby-sitter!"

"Aw, be quiet. Come on, Steve. See! Why you gotta make all my friends laugh for?"

"Ha, ha. Bobby the baby-sitter," my friends said.

"Hey, come on, y'all, let's go play in the park. You comin', Bobby?" one of my friends said.

"Naw, my momma said he can't go in the park cause the last time he went he fell and hurt his knee, with his old stupid self."

And then they left.

"You see? You see! I can't even play with my friends. Man! Come on."

"I'm sorry, Robert. You don't like me, Robert? I'm sorry," Stevie said.

"Aw, be quiet. That's okay," I told him.

One time when my daddy was havin' company

I was just sittin' behind the couch just listenin' to them talk and make jokes and drink beer. And I wasn't makin' no noise. They didn't even know I was there!

Then here comes Stevie with his old loud self. Then when my father heard him, he yelled at *me* and told me to go upstairs.

Just cause of Stevie.

Sometimes people get on your nerves and they don't mean it or nothin' but they just bother you. Why I gotta put up with him? My momma only had one kid. I used to have a lot of fun before old stupid came to live with us.

One Saturday Steve's mother and father came to my house to pick him up like always.

But they said that they were gonna move away and that Stevie wasn't gonna come back anymore.

So then he left. The next mornin' I got up to watch cartoons and I fixed two bowls of corn flakes. Then I just remembered that Stevie wasn't here.

Sometimes we had a lot of fun runnin' in and out of the house. Well, I guess my bed will stay clean from now on. But that wasn't so bad. He couldn't help it cause he was stupid.

I remember the time I ate the last piece of cake in the breadbox and blamed it on him.

We used to play Cowboys and Indians on the stoop.

I remember when I was doin' my homework I used to try to teach him what I had learned. He could write his name pretty good for his age.

I remember the time we played boogie man and we hid under the covers with Daddy's flashlight.

And that time we was playin' in the park under the bushes and we found these two dead rats and one was brown and one was black.

And him and me and my friends used to cook mickies or marshmallows in the park.

We used to have some good times together.

I think he liked my momma better than his own, cause he used to call his mother "Mother" and he called my momma "Mommy."

Aw, no! I let my corn flakes get soggy thinkin' about him.

He was a nice little guy.

He was kinda like a little brother.

Little Stevie.

THE TUB PEOPLE

Written by Pam Conrad
Illustrated by Richard Egielski

Originally published in 1989

The Tub People stood in a line all day on the edge of the bathtub. There were seven of them, and they always stood in the same order—the father, the mother, the grandmother, the doctor, the policeman, the child and the dog.

They were made out of wood, and their faces were very plain. They could smile or frown, or cry or laugh. Sometimes they would even wink at each other, but it hardly showed.

The father of the Tub People liked to play sea captain. He would take the mother, the grandmother and the child for a ride on the floating soap. The others stood on the edge of the tub and waved. Once in a while the child of the Tub People would slide off the soap into the warm bath.

"Help! Help!"

And the captain would rescue him.

"We're coming! We're coming!"

The policeman and the doctor liked to have water races, bobbing from one end of the tub to the other. The child would cheer. The grandmother would say, "Hush! You're very noisy."

When bathtime was over, the Tub People always lined up along the edge of the bathtub—the father, the mother, the grandmother, the doctor, the policeman, the child and the dog.

But one evening the bathwater began rushing down the drain before they were lined up, pulling all the Tub People this way and that. The soap danced over to the drain, turning and turning at the top of a whirlpool. Standing on the soap, getting dizzier and dizzier, was the child of the Tub People.

"Help! Help!"

But this time his father could not save him.

And the Tub Child disappeared down the drain without a sound.

The Tub Mother pressed her face to the grating. She looked and looked for her Tub Child. But she could not see him.

Later that night the Tub People lined up on the edge of the tub, just the six of them. The soap was soft and back in the soap dish. The washcloth made a lonely dripping sound as it hung from the faucet.

The Tub People felt very sad.

The next night the six Tub People climbed onto the washcloth raft. They called and called for their Tub Child. Of course, they knew exactly where their child had gone. But somehow they felt comforted by calling for him.

"Honey, where are you? Come home now. Please come back." But he did not answer.

Every evening the Tub People continued to float in the bathwater. But in time they stopped calling.

And they never winked at each other anymore.

Then an unusual thing happened. The bathwater began going down the drain slower and slower.

Big people came and peered into the tub. "What's the matter with the tub drain?" they asked. They filled the room with deep voices and blocked the light.

"What's the matter with the tub drain?"

The Tub People stood woodenly in their line. If they could have spoken, they would have shouted out what a terrible drain that was, and how it had sucked away their little Tub Child. But they were silent.

That afternoon, a big man came and pried off the drain cover, grunting as he worked. He shone a light down the drain and frowned. Then he pushed in a long wire and jiggled it up and down. Up and down.

"Come home now," the grandmother whispered.

And out of the drain popped the little Tub Child, wet and tired.

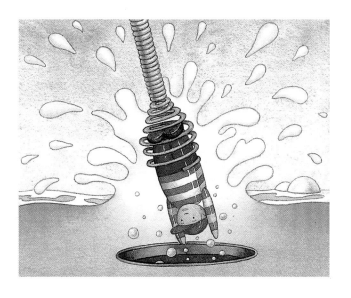

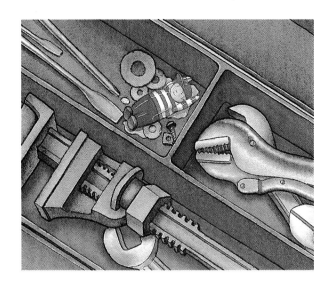

The Tub People stood in a line, quietly watching. One by one they smiled—the father, the mother, the grandmother, the doctor, the policeman and the dog. And the Tub Mother had little soapy tears running down her wooden cheeks.

But the big man did not look at them. He tossed the Tub Child in his toolbox, shut it with a click and left.

The Tub People waited for bathtime, hoping their Tub Child would come back.

But bathtime never came. It grew later and later, and still they waited, worrying all the while.

Finally, when they felt they could wait no longer, they were lifted up and carefully carried into a new room and gently placed on a large, soft bed! It seemed just like the water to them, except that it was dry and very firm.

And there were seven of them once again! The Tub Dog knocked his little wooden head against the Tub Child's head, and very quietly they all laughed.

There was a thick quilt on the bed, and when it was all bunched up, they would go mountain climbing. The father liked to be the leader, and he would lead them up one side of the mountain, and then they would all tumble easily down the other.

The grandmother liked to hide under the pillow and have everyone come find her. The Tub Child liked to fall off the edge and have his father rescue him.

Each night when the lights went out, they lined up along the windowsill, just as they had along the bathtub edge—the father, the mother, the grandmother, the doctor, the policeman, the child and the dog.

But each morning, when the sun came shining in on them, something would be different. The Tub Child would be standing between the Tub Mother and the Tub Father, their sides barely touching.

And if you looked very, very closely, you would see they all had smiles on their small wooden faces.

In Which Pooh Goes Visiting and Gets into a Tight Place

(from WINNIE-THE-POOH)

Written by A. A. Milne

Illustrated by Ernest H. Shepard

Originally published in 1926

Edward Bear, known to his friends as Winnie-the-Pooh, or Pooh for short, was walking through the forest one day, humming proudly to himself. He had made up a little hum that very morning, as he was doing his Stoutness Exercises in front of the glass: *Tra-la-la, tra-la-la,* as he stretched up as high as he could go, and then *Tra-la-la, tra-la—oh, help!—la,* as he tried to reach his toes. After breakfast he had said it over and over to himself until he had learnt it off by heart, and now he was humming it right through, properly. It went like this:

> *Tra-la-la, tra-la-la,*
> *Tra-la-la, tra-la-la,*
> *Rum-tum-tiddle-um-tum.*
> *Tiddle-iddle, tiddle-iddle,*
> *Tiddle-iddle, tiddle-iddle,*
> *Rum-tum-tum-tiddle-um.*

Well, he was humming this hum to himself, and walking along gaily, wondering what everybody else was doing, and what it felt like, being somebody else, when suddenly he came to a sandy bank, and in the bank was a large hole.

"Aha!" said Pooh. (*Rum-tum-tiddle-um-tum.*) "If I know anything about anything, that hole means Rabbit," he said, "and Rabbit means Company," he said, "and Company means Food and Listening-to-Me-Humming and such like. *Rum-tum-tum-tiddle-um.*"

So he bent down, put his head into the hole, and called out:

"Is anybody at home?"

There was a sudden scuffling noise from inside the hole, and then silence.

"What I said was, 'Is anybody at home?'" called out Pooh very loudly.

"No!" said a voice; and then added, "you needn't shout so loud. I heard you quite well the first time."

"Bother!" said Pooh. "Isn't there anybody here at all?"

"Nobody."

Winnie-the-Pooh took his head out of the hole, and thought for a little, and he thought to himself, "There must be somebody there, because somebody must have *said* 'Nobody.'" So he put his head back in the hole, and said:

"Hallo, Rabbit, isn't that you?"

"No," said Rabbit, in a different sort of voice this time.

"But isn't that Rabbit's voice?"

"I don't *think* so," said Rabbit. "It isn't *meant* to be."

"Oh!" said Pooh.

He took his head out of the hole, and had another think, and then he put it back, and said:

"Well, could you very kindly tell me where Rabbit is?"

"He has gone to see his friend Pooh Bear, who is a great friend of his."

"But this *is* Me!" said Bear, very much surprised.

"What sort of Me?"

"Pooh Bear."

"Are you sure?" said Rabbit, still more surprised.

"Quite, quite sure," said Pooh.

"Oh, well, then, come in."

So Pooh pushed and pushed his way through the hole, and at last he got in.

"You were quite right," said Rabbit, looking at him all over. "It *is* you. Glad to see you."

"Who did you think it was?"

"Well, I wasn't sure. You know how it is in the forest. One can't have *anybody* coming into one's house. One has to be *careful*. What about a mouthful of something?"

Pooh always liked a little something at eleven o'clock in the morning, and he was very glad to see Rabbit getting out the plates and mugs; and when Rabbit said, "Honey or condensed milk with your bread?" he was so excited that he said, "Both," and then, so as not to seem greedy, he added, "but don't bother about the bread, please." And for a long time after that he said nothing . . . until at last, humming to himself in a rather sticky voice, he got up, shook Rabbit lovingly by the paw, and said that he must be going on.

"Must you?" said Rabbit politely.

"Well," said Pooh, "I could stay a little longer if it—if you——" and he tried very hard to look in the direction of the larder.

"As a matter of fact," said Rabbit, "I was going out myself directly."

"Oh, well, then, I'll be going on. Good-bye."

"Well, good-bye, if you're sure you won't have any more."

"*Is* there any more?" asked Pooh quickly.

Rabbit took the covers off the dishes, and said no, there wasn't.

"I thought not," said Pooh, nodding to himself. "Well, good-bye. I must be going on."

So he started to climb out of the hole. He pulled with his front paws, and pushed with his back paws, and in a little while his nose was out in the open again . . . and then his ears . . . and then his front paws . . . and then his shoulders . . . and then——

"Oh, help!" said Pooh. "I'd better go back."

"Oh, bother!" said Pooh. "I shall have to go on."

"I can't do either!" said Pooh. "Oh, help *and* bother!"

Now by this time Rabbit wanted to go for a walk too, and finding the front door full, he went out by the back door, and came round to Pooh, and looked at him.

"Hallo, are you stuck?" he asked.

"N-no," said Pooh carelessly. "Just resting

and thinking and humming to myself."

"Here, give us a paw."

Pooh Bear stretched out a paw, and Rabbit pulled and pulled and pulled. . . .

"*Ow!*" cried Pooh. "You're hurting!"

"The fact is," said Rabbit, "you're stuck."

"It all comes," said Pooh crossly, "of not having front doors big enough."

"It all comes," said Rabbit sternly, "of eating too much. I thought at the time," said Rabbit, "only I didn't like to say anything," said Rabbit, "and I knew it wasn't *me*," he said. "Well, well, I shall go and fetch Christopher Robin."

Christopher Robin lived at the other end of the Forest, and when he came back with Rabbit, and saw the front half of Pooh, he said, "Silly old Bear," in such a loving voice that everybody felt quite hopeful again.

"I was just beginning to think," said Bear, sniffing slightly, "that Rabbit might never be able to use his front door again. And I should *hate* that," he said.

"So should I," said Rabbit.

"Use his front door again?" said Christopher Robin. "Of course he'll use his front door again."

"Good," said Rabbit.

"If we can't pull you out, Pooh, we might push you back."

Rabbit scratched his whiskers thoughtfully, and pointed out that, when once Pooh was pushed back, he was back, and of course nobody was more glad to see Pooh than *he* was, still there it was, some lived in trees and some lived underground, and——

"You mean I'd *never* get out?" said Pooh.

"I mean," said Rabbit, "that having got *so* far, it seems a pity to waste it."

Christopher Robin nodded.

"Then there's only one thing to be done," he said. "We shall have to wait for you to get thin again."

"How long does getting thin take?" asked Pooh anxiously.

"About a week, I should think."

"But I can't stay here for a *week!*"

"You can *stay* here all right, silly old Bear. It's getting you out which is so difficult."

"We'll read to you," said Rabbit cheerfully. "And I hope it won't snow," he added. "And I say, old fellow, you're taking up a good deal of room in my house—*do* you mind if I use your back legs as a towel-horse? Because, I mean, there they are—doing nothing—and it would be very convenient just to hang the towels on them."

"A week!" said Pooh gloomily. *"What about meals?"*

"I'm afraid no meals," said Christopher Robin, "because of getting thin quicker. But we *will* read to you."

Bear began to sigh, and then found he couldn't because he was so tightly stuck; and a tear rolled down his eye, as he said:

"Then would you read a Sustaining Book, such as would help and comfort a Wedged Bear in Great Tightness?"

So for a week Christopher Robin read that sort of book at the North end of Pooh,

and Rabbit hung his washing on the South end . . .

and in between Bear felt himself getting slenderer and slenderer. And at the end of the week Christopher Robin said, *"Now!"*

So he took hold of Pooh's front paws and
Rabbit took hold of Christopher Robin, and all
Rabbit's friends and relations took hold of
Rabbit, and they all pulled together. . . .

And for a long time Pooh only said
"*Ow!*" . . .

And "*Oh!*" . . .

And then, all of a sudden, he said "*Pop!*"
just as if a cork were coming out of a bottle.

And Christopher Robin and Rabbit and all
Rabbit's friends and relations went head-over-
heels backwards . . . and on top of them came
Winnie-the-Pooh—free!

So, with a nod of thanks to his friends, he
went on with his walk through the forest,
humming proudly to himself. But, Christopher
Robin looked after him lovingly, and said to
himself, "Silly old Bear!"

BEDTIME FOR FRANCES

Written by Russell Hoban
Illustrated by Garth Williams

Originally published in 1960

The big hand of the clock is at 12.
The little hand is at 7.
It is seven o'clock.
It is bedtime for Frances.
Mother said, "It is time for bed."
Father said, "It is time for bed."
Frances said, "I want a glass of milk."
"All right," said Father.
"All right," said Mother.
"You may have a glass of milk."
Frances drank the milk.

"Carry me to my room, Father," said Frances.

"All right," said Father.

"Piggyback," said Frances.

So Father carried her piggyback to her room.

Father kissed Frances good night.

Mother kissed Frances good night.

Frances said, "May I sleep with my teddy bear?"

Father gave her the teddy bear.

Frances said, "May I sleep with my doll, too?"

Mother gave her the doll.

"Good night," said Father.

"Good night," said Mother.

"Did you kiss me?" said Frances.

"Yes," said Mother.

"Yes," said Father.

"Kiss me again," said Frances.

Father kissed her again.

Mother kissed her again.

They closed the door.

"May I have my door open?" said Frances.

Father opened the door.

"Good night," said Mother.

"Good night," said Father.

"Good night," said Frances.

Frances could not sleep.

She closed her eyes, but she still could not sleep.

So she began to sing a little song about the alphabet.

She made it up as she went along:

"A is for apple pie,

B is for bear,

C is for crocodile, combing his hair.

D is for dumplings . . ."

Frances kept singing through E, F, G, H, I, J, K, L, M, N, O,

P, Q, and R, and she had no trouble until

she got near the end of the alphabet.

"S is for sailboat,

T is for tiger,

U is for underwear, down in the drier . . ."

Frances stopped because "drier" did not sound like "tiger."

She started to think about tigers.

She thought about big tigers and little tigers,

baby tigers and mother and father tigers,

sister tigers and brother tigers,

aunt tigers and uncle tigers.

"I wonder if there are any tigers around here," she said.

Frances looked around her room.

She thought maybe she could see a tiger in the corner.

She was not afraid, but she wanted to be sure.

So she looked again.

She was sure she could see a tiger.

She went to tell Mother and Father.

"There is a tiger in my room," said Frances.

"Did he bite you?" said Father.

"No," said Frances.

"Did he scratch you?" said Mother.

"No," said Frances.

"Then he is a friendly tiger," said Father.

"He will not hurt you. Go back to sleep."

"Do I have to?" said Frances.

"Yes," said Father.

"Yes," said Mother.

Father kissed her.

Mother kissed her.

Frances went back to bed, and finished her song on the way.

She closed her eyes again.

She still could not sleep.

Frances opened her eyes and looked around.

She saw something big and dark.

"Giants are big and dark," she thought.

"Maybe that is a giant.

I think it *is* a giant.

I think that giant wants to get me."

She went into the living room.

Mother and Father were watching television
and having tea and cake.

Frances said, "There is a giant in my room.

May I watch television?"

"No," said Mother.

"No," said Father.

Frances said, "The giant wants to get me.

May I have some cake?"

Father gave Frances a piece of cake.

Father said, "How do you know he wants to get you?"

Frances said, "Isn't that what giants do?"

Father said, "Not always. Why don't you ask him what he wants?"

Frances went back to her room.

She went right over to the giant.

She said, "What do you want, Giant?"

She took a good look at him.

There was no giant.

It was just the chair and her bathrobe.

So she went to bed again.

Frances was not very tired and did not close her eyes.

She looked up at the ceiling.

There was a crack in the ceiling, and she thought about it.

"Maybe something will come out of that crack," she thought.

"Maybe bugs or spiders. Maybe something with a lot of skinny legs in the dark."

She went to get Father. He was brushing his teeth.

Frances said, "Something scary is going to come out of the crack in the ceiling. I forgot to brush my teeth."

Father said, "You brush your teeth, and I will have a look."

Frances brushed her teeth.

Father came back and said, "Nothing could come out of such a little crack. But if you are worried about it, get somebody to help you watch. You can take turns."

Frances told her teddy bear to watch.

They took turns for a while.

Then Frances got tired of it and let Teddy do all the watching.

Frances got up and went to the bathroom.

When she came back she was not sleepy at all.

The window was open and the wind was blowing the curtains.

"I do not like the way those curtains are moving," said Frances.

"Maybe there is *something* waiting, very soft and quiet. Maybe it moves the curtains just to see if I am watching."

She went into Mother and Father's room to tell them.

They were asleep.

Frances stood by Father's side of the bed very quietly,
right near his head.

She was so quiet that she was the quietest thing in the room.

She was so quiet that Father woke up all of a sudden,
with his eyes wide open.

He said, "Umph!"

Frances said, "There is something moving the curtains.
May I sleep with you?"

Father said, "Listen, Frances, do you want to know
why the curtains are moving?"

"Why?" said Frances.

"That is the wind's job," said Father. "Every night the wind
has to go around and blow all the curtains."

"How can the wind have a job?" said Frances.

"*Everybody* has a job," said Father.

"I have to go to my office every morning at nine o'clock.

That is my job. You have to go to sleep

so you can be wide awake for school tomorrow.

That is *your* job."

Frances said, "I know, but . . ."

Father said, "I have not finished.

If the wind does not blow the curtains, he will be out of a job.

If I do not go to the office, I will be out of a job.

And if you do not go to sleep now,

do you know what will happen to you?"

"I will be out of a job?" said Frances.

"No," said Father.

"I will get a spanking?" said Frances.

"Right!" said Father.

"Good night!" said Frances, and she went back to her room.

Frances closed the window and got into bed.

Suddenly there was a noise at the window.

She heard BUMP! and THUMP!

"I *know* something will get me this time," she thought.

She jumped out of bed and went to tell Mother and Father.

When she got to their door, she thought about it some more
and decided not to tell them.

She went back to her room.

Frances heard the noise at the window again.

She pulled the covers over her head.

"I wonder what it is," she thought.

"If it is something *very* bad, Father will *have* to come
and chase it away."

She pulled off the covers and stood on her bed
so she could look out the window.

She saw a moth bumping against the window.

Bump and thump.

His wings smacked the glass.

Whack and smack!

Whack and smack made Frances think of a spanking.

And all of a sudden she was tired.
She lay down and closed her eyes
so she could think better. She thought,
"There were so many giants and tigers
and scary and exciting things before,
that I am pretty tired now.
That is just a moth, and he is only doing his job,
the same as the wind.
His job is bumping and thumping,
and my job is to sleep."
So she went to sleep
and did not get out of bed again
until Mother called her for breakfast.

THE STINKY CHEESE MAN

(from THE STINKY CHEESE MAN AND OTHER FAIRLY STUPID TALES)

Written by Jon Scieszka
Illustrated by Lane Smith

Originally published in 1992

Once upon a time there was a little old woman and a little old man who lived together in a little old house.

They were lonely.

So the little old lady decided to make a man out of stinky cheese.

She gave him a piece of bacon for a mouth and two olives for eyes and put him in the oven to cook.

When she opened the oven to see if he was done, the smell knocked her back. "Phew! What is that terrible smell?" she cried. The Stinky Cheese Man hopped out of the oven and ran out the door calling, "Run run run as fast as you can. You can't catch me. I'm the Stinky Cheese Man!"

The little old lady and the little old man sniffed the air. "I'm not really very hungry," said the little old man.

"I'm not really all that lonely," said the little old lady. So they didn't chase the Stinky Cheese Man.

The Stinky Cheese Man ran and ran until he met a cow eating grass in a field. "Wow! What's that awful smell?" said the cow.

The Stinky Cheese Man said, "I've run away from a little old lady and a little old man and I can run away from you too I can. Run run run as fast as you can. You can't catch me. I'm the Stinky Cheese Man!"

The cow gave another sniff and said, "I'll bet you could give someone two or three stomachaches. I think I'll just eat weeds."

So the cow didn't chase the Stinky Cheese Man either.

The Stinky Cheese Man ran and ran until he met some kids playing outside school.

"Gross," said a little girl. "What's that nasty smell?"

"I've run away from a little old lady, and a little old man, and a cow, and I can run away from you too I can. Run run run as fast as you can. You can't catch me. I'm the Stinky Cheese Man!"

A little boy looked up, sniffed the air, and said, "If we catch him, our teacher will probably make us eat him. Let's get out of here."

So the kids didn't chase the Stinky Cheese Man either.

By and by the Stinky Cheese Man came to a river with no bridge.

"How will I ever cross this river? It's too big to jump, and if I try to swim across I'll probably fall apart," said You-Know-Who.

Just then the sly fox (who shows up in a lot of stories like these) poked his head out of the bushes.

"Why, just hop on my back and I'll carry you across, Stinky Cheese Man."

"How do I know you won't eat me?"

"Trust me," said the fox.

So the Stinky Cheese Man hopped on the fox's back.

The fox swam to the middle of the river and said, "Oh man! What is that funky smell?"

The fox coughed, gagged, and sneezed, and the Stinky Cheese Man flew off his back and into the river where he fell apart.

The End.

THE STORY OF BABAR

Written and illustrated by Jean de Brunhoff

Originally published in 1933

In the great forest a little elephant is born. His name is Babar. His mother loves him very much. She rocks him to sleep with her trunk while singing softly to him.

Babar has grown bigger. He now plays with the other little elephants. He is a very good little elephant. See him digging in the sand with his shell.

Babar is riding happily on his mother's back, when a wicked hunter, hidden behind some bushes, shoots at them.

The hunter has killed Babar's mother! The monkey hides, the birds fly away, Babar cries. The hunter runs up to catch poor Babar.

Babar runs away because he is afraid of the hunter. After several days, very tired indeed, he comes to a town…

He hardly knows what to make of it because this is the first time that he has seen so many houses.

So many things are new to him! The broad streets! The automobiles and noises! However, he is especially interested in two gentlemen he notices on the street.

He says to himself: "Really they are very well dressed. I would like to have some fine clothes, too! I wonder how I can get them?"

Luckily, a very rich old lady who has always been fond of little elephants understands right away that he is longing for a fine suit. As she likes to make people happy, she gives him her purse.

Babar says to her politely: "Thank you, Madam."

Without wasting any time, Babar goes into a big store. He enters the elevator. It is such fun to ride up and down in this funny box, that he rides all the way up ten times and all the way down ten times. He did not want to stop but the elevator boy finally said to him: "This is not a toy, Mr. Elephant. You must get out and do your shopping. Look, here is the floorwalker."

Babar then buys himself: a shirt with a collar and tie, a suit of a becoming shade of green, then a handsome derby hat, and also shoes with spats.

Well satisfied with his purchases and feeling very elegant indeed, Babar now goes to the photographer to have his picture taken.

And here is his photograph.

Babar dines with his friend the old lady. She thinks he looks very smart in his new clothes. After dinner, because he is tired, he goes to bed and falls asleep very quickly.

Babar now lives at the old lady's house. In the mornings, he does setting-up exercises with her, and then he takes his bath.

He goes out for an automobile ride every day. The old lady has given him the car. She gives him whatever he wants.

A learned professor gives him lessons. Babar pays attention and does well in his work. He is a good pupil and makes rapid progress.

In the evening, after dinner, he tells the old lady's friends all about his life in the great forest.

However, Babar is not quite happy, for he misses playing in the great forest with his little cousins and his friends the monkeys.

He often stands at the window, thinking sadly of his childhood, and cries when he remembers his mother.

Two years have passed. One day during his walk he sees two little elephants coming toward him. They have no clothes on. "Why," he says in astonishment to the old lady, "it's Arthur and Céleste, my little cousins!"

Babar kisses them affectionately and hurries off with them to buy them some fine clothes.

He takes them to a pastry shop to eat some good cakes.

Meanwhile, in the forest, the elephants are calling and hunting high and low for Arthur and Céleste, and their mothers are very worried. Fortunately, in flying over the town, an old marabou bird has seen them and comes back quickly to tell the news.

The mothers of Arthur and Céleste have come to the town to fetch them. They are very happy to have them back, but they scold them just the same because they ran away.

Babar makes up his mind to go back with Arthur and Céleste and their mothers to see the great forest again. The old lady helps him to pack his trunk.

They are all ready to start. Babar kisses the old lady good-bye. He would be quite happy to go if it were not for leaving her. He promises to come back some day. He will never forget her.

They have gone…There is no room in the car for the mothers, so they run behind, and lift up their trunks to avoid breathing the dust. The old lady is left alone. Sadly she wonders: "When shall I see my little Babar again?"

Alas, that very day, the King of the elephants had eaten a bad mushroom.

It poisoned him and he became ill, so ill that he died. This was a great calamity.

After the funeral the three oldest elephants were holding a meeting to choose a new King.

Just then they hear a noise, they turn around. Guess what they see! Babar arriving in his car, and all the elephants running and shouting: "Here they are! Here they are! Hello Babar! Hello Arthur! Hello Céleste! What beautiful clothes! What a beautiful car!"

Then Cornelius, the oldest of all the elephants, spoke in his quavering voice: "My good friends, we are seeking a King, why not choose Babar? He has just returned from the big city, he has learned so much living among men, let us crown him King." All the other elephants thought that Cornelius had spoken wisely—and eagerly they await Babar's reply.

"I want to thank you one and all," said Babar, "but before accepting your proposal, I must explain to you that, while we were traveling in the car, Céleste and I became engaged. If I become your King, she will be your Queen."

"Long live Queen Céleste! Long live King Babar!!!" cry all the elephants

without a moment's hesitation. And thus it was that Babar became King.

"You have good ideas," said Babar to Cornelius, "I will therefore make you a general, and when I get my crown, I will give you my hat. In a week I shall marry Céleste. We will then have a splendid party in honor of our marriage and our coronation." Then turning to the birds, Babar asks them to go and invite all the animals to the festivities, and he tells the dromedary to go to the town and buy some beautiful wedding clothes.

The wedding guests begin to arrive. The dromedary returns with the bridal costumes just in the nick of time for the ceremony.

After the wedding and the coronation, everybody dances merrily.

The festivities are over, night has fallen, the stars have risen in the sky. King Babar and Queen Céleste are indeed very happy.

Now the world is asleep. The guests have gone home—happy, though tired from too much dancing. They will long remember this great celebration.

And now King Babar and Queen Céleste, both eager for further adventures, set out on their honeymoon in a gorgeous yellow balloon.

THE BERENSTAIN BEARS AND THE SPOOKY OLD TREE

Written and illustrated by Stan and Jan Berenstain

Originally published in 1978

Three little bears.
One with a light.
One with a stick.
One with a rope.

A spooky old tree.
Do they dare go into
that spooky old tree?

Yes.
They dare.

Three little bears . . .
One with a light.
One with a stick.
One with a rope.

192

A twisty old stair.
Do they dare go up
that twisty old stair?

Yes.
They dare.

Three little bears.
One with a light.
One with a stick.
And <u>one</u> with the shivers.

A giant key.

A moving wall.

Will the three little bears
go through that wall?
Do they dare go into
that spooky old hall?

Yes.
They dare.

Three little bears.
One with a light.
And <u>two</u> with the shivers.

Great Sleeping Bear.
Do they dare go over
Great Sleeping Bear?
Do they dare?
Well . . .
They came into the tree.
They climbed the stair.
They went through the wall . . .
and into the hall.
So of course they went over
Great Sleeping Bear!

Three little bears . . .
without a light,
without a stick,
without a rope.
And <u>all</u> with the shivers!
How will they ever
get out of there?

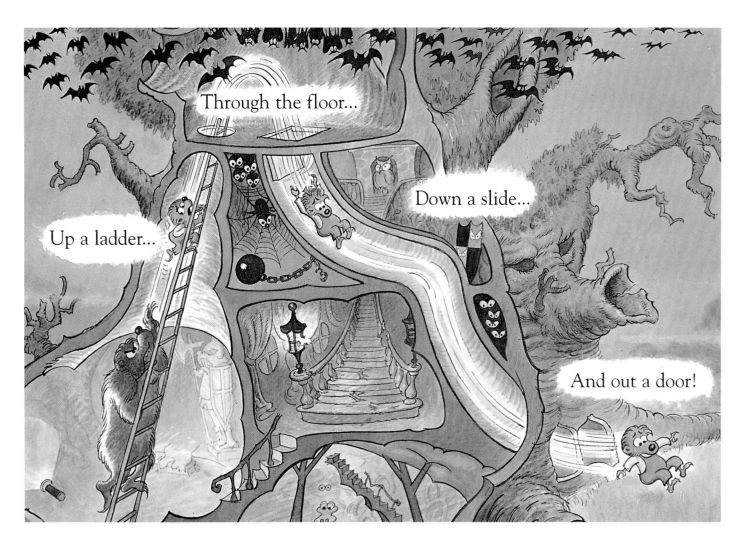

Three little bears
running fast.
Home again.
Safe at last.

THE ELVES IN THE SHELVES

(from A NECKLACE OF RAINDROPS)

Written by Joan Aiken

Illustrated by Jan Pieńkowski

Originally published in 1968

There was a little girl called Janet, and it was her birthday. She had lots of presents. A little red bicycle. And a pair of roller-skates. And a skipping-rope. And a big pile of books. But just the same, Janet was not very happy.

Why? Because her mother was away, visiting her sick granny. And her daddy, who was a train-driver, had to go off and drive his train. And so Janet would be all alone that night.

Her daddy gave her a very nice supper—bread and butter and brown sugar and a drink of creamy milk. Then he tucked her up in bed and said, "Shut your eyes and go to sleep, and in no time at all it will be tomorrow and I shall be home for breakfast." Off he went to drive his train.

Janet shut her eyes, but then she opened them again. She did not like being all alone.

"Oh," sighed Janet, "I wish I had someone to talk to."

Then she heard a queer noise. What could it be? Pitter-patter, tip-tap, scuffle-scuffle, rattle-rattle, pitter-patter. Janet listened. The noise came from the next room. There it was again! Pitter-patter, tip-tap, scuffle-scuffle, rattle-rattle, pitter-patter. Janet jumped out of bed and tiptoed to the next room.

What do you think she saw?

All her new books were opening, and all the creatures in them were coming out. There was a book about elves, and all the elves were running out of the book and playing leap-frog and climbing up into the china closet. There was a book about mermaids, and all the mermaids were swimming out and diving into the bath. There was a book about penguins, and all the penguins were wad-dling out and climbing up into the ice-box. There was a book about seals, and all the seals were flop-ping out and pulling each other up into the sink.

So when Janet looked, she saw

elves in the shelves,
   mermaids in the bathtub,
      penguins in the ice-box,
         rabbits in the coal-bin,
           peacocks on the table and
              seals in the sink.

Wasn't that a funny sight, enough to make you blink!

"*Who* are all of you?" said Janet. "And *what* are you doing here?"

"We have come to play with you so you shan't be all alone!"

Janet had never had so many playmates before. Who should she play with first? The elves in the shelves? They were playing football with a marble. Or the mermaids in the bathtub? They were floating on Janet's sponge for a raft. Or the penguins in the ice-box? They were sliding on a slippery bit of ice. Or the rabbits in the coal-bin? They were playing hunt-the-thimble. Or the peacocks on the table? They were playing patience. Or the seals in the sink? There were playing splashing.

First Janet played with the elves. Then with the mermaids. Then with the penguins. Then with the rabbits. Then with the peacocks. Then with the seals.

Then she heard a voice behind her. It said, "Nobody wants to play with *me!*"

Janet looked round. There stood a tiger in front of the fire. He had come out of the very bottom book of all. He was big, and he had long, long whiskers and a long, long tail, and he had black and yellow stripes all over.

"Tickle my tail!" he said, "and I'll chase you!"

"We don't like to be chased," cried the elves. "You're too rough." But he chased the elves along the shelves.

"We don't like to be chased," cried the mermaids. But Tiger chased them out of the bathtub.

"We don't want to be chased," cried the penguins. But Tiger chased them out of the ice-box.

"We don't want to be chased," squeaked the rabbits. But Tiger chased them out of the coal-bin.

"We don't want to be chased," barked the seals. But Tiger chased them out of the sink.

"We don't want to be chased," screamed the peacocks. But Tiger chased them off the table.

Everyone was cross, and some of the elves were crying.

"Tiger," said Janet, "you are too rough. You must play more gently."

"Tell him to go back into his book!" everybody cried.

So Janet picked up the book and said, "Bad boy! Bad Tiger! Go back inside!"

Tiger looked sad. "I only want to run," he said. "For I can run

faster than the wind,
   faster than the weather,
      faster than the fastest clouds
         that cross the sky together!

Please," Tiger said to Janet, "can I go for a run outside? After that I will be quiet and good, and not chase the others."

"I had better come too," Janet said, "to keep an eye on you."

"Then jump on my back and tickle my tail!"

So Janet jumped on his back and tickled his tail. And he ran out of the door and down the stairs and along the street and across the park, fast, faster, fastest of all! And as he ran he sang,

"I can run
   faster than the wind,
      faster than the weather,
         faster than the fastest clouds
           that cross the sky together!"

Then they met a man with a glass foot. He cried,

"Oh, please, my hat has blown off. Can you catch it for me, for if I run I might break my glass foot."

"Pooh!" said Tiger. "I can easily catch your hat."

And he went *chasing* across the park and they caught the hat and gave it back to the man with the glass foot. And he was very grateful.

Then they saw a woman who called, "Please, can you help me? I belong in Tomorrow, but I got left behind. Can you catch up with Tomorrow for me?"

"Easy," said Tiger. "For I can run

faster than the wind,
  faster than the weather,
    faster than the fastest clouds
      that cross the sky together!

Jump on my back behind Janet and tickle my tail."

So the woman jumped on his back and she tickled his tail. And he went *chasing* over the country and easily caught up with Tomorrow and put the woman back where she belonged.

"Thank you," she called. "I'll send you a postcard from Tomorrow."

Then they saw a boy who called, "Help! A Pandaconda from the circus is chasing me

because I pulled its whiskers. Save me!"

"Easy!" said Tiger. "Jump on my back and tickle my tail."

So they tickled his tail and away he went, fast, faster, fastest of all! At first the Pandaconda came whistling after, but soon it gave up and went back to sleep in its hole under the merry-go-round.

"Thank you for saving me," said the boy. And he gave them each a nut and jumped off as they passed by his home.

Then Janet said, "*Goodness*, there's the train that my daddy comes home on. Quick, quick, or he'll be home first and wonder where I am!"

"Easy!" said Tiger. "I can beat a train any day. For I can run

faster than the wind,
  faster than the weather,
    faster than the fastest clouds
      that cross the sky together!

Only tickle my tail." So Janet tickled his tail and they went *racing* back, over the country and over the town, over houses and churches and mountains and rivers, across the park and along the street, and in at Janet's window.

"Quick!" she cried. "You must all get into your books, for my daddy's coming home."

For there were

elves in the shelves,
   mermaids in the bathtub,
      penguins in the ice-box,
         rabbits in the coal-bin,
            peacocks on the table and
               seals in the sink.

"I will play with you all again tomorrow night," Janet promised. She pushed them all into their books (Tiger was the hardest to push because he was so big) and then she ran next door and jumped into bed and shut her eyes tight.

Next thing, she was asleep!

And next thing she was awake again, and there was her daddy making breakfast. After breakfast, Janet went and looked at her books, but they were quite quiet and still. If it hadn't been for a small, just the *smallest* footprint on a shelf, a little, just the *littlest* gold scale in the bathtub, a tiny, just the *tiniest* feather in the ice-box, and ONE tiger's whisker on the rug, you would never have guessed that there had been

elves in the shelves,
   mermaids in the bathtub,
      penguins in the ice-box,
         rabbits in the coal-bin,
            peacocks on the table,
               seals in the sink

and a big stripy tiger sitting in front of the fire...

Ten, Nine, Eight

Written and illustrated by Molly Bang

Originally published in 1983

10 small toes all washed and warm

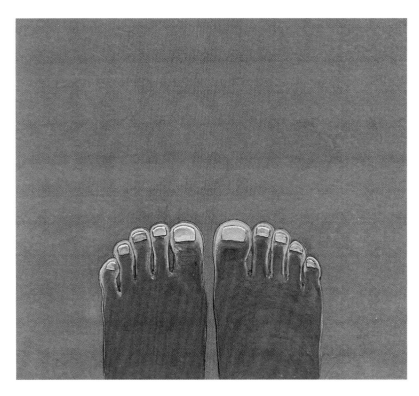

9 soft friends
in a quiet room

8 square windowpanes
with falling snow

7 empty shoes in a short
straight row

204

6 pale seashells
hanging down

5 round buttons on
a yellow gown

4 sleepy eyes which open and close

3 loving kisses on cheeks and nose

2 strong arms around
a fuzzy bear's head

1 big girl all ready
for bed

STELLALUNA

Written and illustrated by Janell Cannon

Originally published in 1993

The hero of this story is a fruit bat. Unlike most bats, which navigate by echolocation, fruit bats depend on their keen vision and sense of smell to navigate. The original book includes scientific information about all kinds of bats in an afterword that children will find fascinating.

In a warm and sultry forest far, far away, there once lived a mother fruit bat and her new baby.

Oh, how Mother Bat loved her soft tiny baby. "I'll name you Stellaluna," she crooned.

Each night, Mother Bat would carry Stellaluna clutched to her breast as she flew out to search for food.

One night, as Mother Bat followed the heavy scent of ripe fruit, an owl spied her. On silent wings the powerful bird swooped down upon the bats.

Dodging and shrieking, Mother Bat tried to escape, but the owl struck again and again, knocking Stellaluna into the air. Her baby wings were as limp and useless as wet paper.

Down, down she went, faster and faster, into the forest below.

The dark leafy tangle of branches caught Stellaluna as she fell. One twig was small enough for Stellaluna's tiny feet. Wrapping her wings about her, she clutched the thin branch, trembling with cold and fear.

"Mother," Stellaluna squeaked. "Where are you?"

By daybreak, the baby bat could hold on no longer. Down, down again she dropped.

Flump! Stellaluna landed headfirst in a soft downy nest, startling the three baby birds who lived there.

Stellaluna quickly clambered from the nest and hung out of sight below it. She listened to the babble of the three birds.

"What was *that?*" cried Flap.

"I don't know, but it's hanging by its feet," chirped Flitter.

"Shhh! Here comes Mama," hissed Pip.

Many, many times that day Mama Bird flew away, always returning with food for her babies.

Stellaluna was terribly hungry—but *not* for the crawly things Mama Bird brought.

Finally, though, the little bat could bear it no longer. She climbed into the nest, closed her eyes, and opened her mouth.

Plop! In dropped a big green grasshopper!

Stellaluna learned to be like the birds. She stayed awake all day and slept at night. She ate bugs even though they tasted awful. Her bat ways were quickly disappearing. Except for one thing: Stellaluna still liked to sleep hanging by her feet.

Once, when Mama was away, the curious baby birds decided to try it, too. When Mama Bird came home she saw eight tiny feet gripping the edge of the nest.

"Eeeek!" she cried. "Get back up here this instant! You're going to fall and break your necks!"

The birds clambered back into the nest, but Mama Bird stopped Stellaluna. "You are teaching my children to do bad things. I will not let you back into this nest unless you promise to obey all the rules of this house."

Stellaluna promised. She ate bugs without making faces. She slept in the nest at night. And she didn't hang by her feet. Stellaluna behaved as a good bird should.

All the babies grew quickly. Soon the nest became crowded.

Mama Bird told them it was time to learn to fly. One by one, Pip, Flitter, Flap, and Stellaluna jumped from the nest.

Their wings worked!

I'm just like them, thought Stellaluna. I can fly, too.

Pip, Flitter, and Flap landed gracefully on a branch.

Stellaluna tried to do the same.

How embarrassing!

I will fly all day, Stellaluna told herself. Then no one will see how clumsy I am.

The next day, Pip, Flitter, Flap, and Stellaluna went flying far from home. They flew for hours, exercising their new wings.

"The sun is setting," warned Flitter.

"We had better go home or we will get lost in the dark," said Flap.

But Stellaluna had flown far ahead and was nowhere to be seen. The three anxious birds went home without her.

All alone, Stellaluna flew and flew until her wings ached and she dropped into a tree. "I promised not to hang by my feet," Stellaluna sighed. So she hung by her thumbs and soon fell asleep.

She didn't hear the soft sound of wings coming near.

"Hey!" a loud voice said. "Why are you hanging upside down?"

Stellaluna's eyes opened wide. She saw a most peculiar face. "I'm not upside down, *you* are!" Stellaluna said.

"Ah, but you're a *bat*. Bats hang by their feet. You are hanging by your thumbs, so that makes you *upside down!*" the creature said. "I'm a bat. I am hanging by my feet. That makes me *right side up!*"

Stellaluna was confused. "Mama Bird told me I was upside down. She said I was wrong…"

"Wrong for a bird, maybe, but not for a bat."

More bats gathered around to see the strange young bat who behaved like a bird. Stellaluna told them her story.

"You ate *b-bugs?*" stuttered one.

"You slept at *night?*" gasped another.

"How very strange," they all murmured.

"Wait! Wait! Let me look at this child." A bat pushed through the crowd. "An *owl* attacked you?" she asked. Sniffing Stellaluna's fur, she whispered, "You are *Stellaluna*. You are my baby."

"You escaped the owl?" cried Stellaluna. "You survived?"

"Yes," said Mother Bat as she wrapped her wings around Stellaluna. "Come with me and I'll show you where to find the most delicious fruit. You'll never have to eat another bug as long as you live."

"But it's nighttime," Stellaluna squeaked. "We can't fly in the dark or we will crash into trees."

"We're bats," said Mother Bat. "We can see in darkness. Come with us."

Stellaluna was afraid, but she let go of the tree and dropped into the deep blue sky.

Stellaluna *could* see. She felt as though rays of light shone from her eyes. She was able to see everything in her path.

Soon the bats found a mango tree, and Stellaluna ate as much of the fruit as she could hold.

"I'll never eat another bug as long as I live," cheered Stellaluna as she stuffed herself full. "I must tell Pip, Flitter, and Flap!"

The next day Stellaluna went to visit the birds.

"Come with me and meet my bat family," said Stellaluna.

"Okay, let's go," agreed Pip.

"They hang by their feet and they fly at night and they eat the best food in the world," Stellaluna explained to the birds on the way.

212

As the birds flew among the bats, Flap said, "I feel upside down here."

So the birds hung by their feet.

"Wait until dark," Stellaluna said excitedly. "We will fly at night."

When night came Stellaluna flew away. Pip. Flitter, and Flap leapt from the tree to follow her.

"I can't see a thing!" yelled Pip.

"Neither can I," howled Flitter.

"Aaeee!" shrieked Flap.

"They're going to crash," gasped Stellaluna. "I must rescue them!"

Stellaluna swooped about, grabbing her friends in the air. She lifted them to a tree, and the birds grasped a branch. Stellaluna hung from the limb above them.

"We're safe," said Stellaluna. Then she sighed. "I wish you could see in the dark, too."

"We wish you could land on your feet," Flitter replied. Pip and Flap nodded.

They perched in silence for a long time.

"How can we be so different and feel so much alike?" mused Flitter.

"And how can we feel so different and be so much alike?" wondered Pip.

"I think this is quite a mystery," Flap chirped.

"I agree," said Stellaluna. "But we're friends. And that's a fact."

D.W. THE PICKY EATER

Written and illustrated by Marc Brown

Originally published in 1995

D.W. and her brother, Arthur, were helping Mother unpack the groceries. "Yuck!" said D.W. "I'm not going to eat this!"

"You've never even tried it," said mother.

"It's looking at me," said D.W.

"I don't eat anything with eyes, or pickles, tomatoes, mushrooms, eggplant, pineapple, parsnips, and cauliflower. Well . . . and maybe a few other things. I would never eat liver in a million years, and more than anything else in the whole world, I hate spinach!"

"Face it," said Arthur. "You are a picky eater."

On Wednesday, Father surprised D.W. when he packed her lunch for play group.

"Did you eat your sandwich?" he asked on the way home.

"It fell in the dirt," said D.W. "It was an accident."

Thursday at dinner, D.W. pretended to try the Hawaiian shrimp.

"I saw that," whispered Arthur.

214

Emily invited D.W. to stay for dinner on Friday.

"We're having spaghetti!" said Emily.

"May I have mine plain, please?" asked D.W. "No sauce."

"That's the best part!" said Emily.

"Are these little green things spinach?" D.W. asked when her spaghetti arrived.

"It's parsley," said Emily. "Try it."

While everyone else ate, D.W. just moved her food back and forth into little piles.

"You'll never be a Clean Plate Ranger at this rate," said Emily.

On Saturday, D.W. and her family went out to eat.

"This salad has spinach in it!" cried D.W.

"Just try it," said Mother.

"She's going to have a tantrum," warned Arthur.

"Please try it," said Father.

"No!" said D.W., and she pounded her fist into the salad dish.

"I'm so embarrassed," said Mother.

"No more restaurants for you," scolded Father.

From then on, the family went out to dinner without D.W.

"I'd rather stay home with a sitter anyway," said D.W.

Mrs. Cross only allowed carrot sticks for snacks. And at exactly eight o'clock she said, "Bedtime. Now march, quick like a bunny!"

One morning at breakfast, Arthur twirled a tiny paper umbrella.

"Where did you get that?" demanded D.W.

"At the Chinese restaurant," said Arthur. "It was fun!"

D.W. began to wonder what she was missing.

"Tomorrow is Grandma Thora's birthday," announced Mother. "Our big night out!"

"I want to go, too!" said D.W.

"You will have to eat what's on the menu," said Father.

"I will," said D.W.

"You will have to try new foods," said Mother.

"I will," said D.W.

"Even if it's green and looks like a leaf?" asked Arthur.

Everyone got dressed up Saturday night. D.W wore her black shoes with the bows, even though they pinched her toes.

"Happy Birthday, Grandma Thora!" said Arthur and D.W. together.

"I hope they have plain spaghetti," prayed D.W.

D.W. was happy when she sat in her chair. "No one will see me if I have to get rid of something disgusting," she thought.

"I'm Richard," said the waiter. "Here's a kiddie seat for the little lady."

"Thanks a lot," said D.W.

"Do you have food with little umbrellas on it?" she asked.

"We do not," said the waiter.

216

Everyone ordered except D.W.

"You'd better bring her the kiddie menu," said Arthur.

Father read D.W. the menu.

"Time to choose," he said.

"I guess I'll have the Little Bo Peep Pot Pie," said D.W.

When dinner was served, all eyes were on D.W.

She took a bite.

"This is good!" said D.W.

D.W. took another bite and another.

She drank all her milk.

"Good work!" said Mother and Father.

"I'm very proud of you," said Grandma Thora.

Arthur checked under the table. "Where'd you put it?" he asked.

"I could eat this every night," said D.W. "Will you make it for me at home? Please?"

"I'll need the recipe," said Mother.

"What a good little eater," said the waiter when he cleared D.W.'s dishes.

"It was delicious," said D.W. "How do you make that?"

"Very simple, really," said the waiter. "Just take some pie pastry and fill it with . . ."

". . . lots and lots of spinach!"

PETUNIA

Written and illustrated by Roger Duvoisin

Originally published in 1950

In the meadow, early one morning, Petunia, the silly goose, went strolling. She ate a bug here, clipped off a clover leaf there, and she picked at the dewdrops on the goldenrod leaves.

Then, suddenly, she saw something she had never seen before in the meadow. What was it?

Petunia stole closer and closer and sniffed at it from all sides. "By Goosey Gander," she said, "it does not smell like food for a goose. But I believe I have seen such a thing before. . . .

"Yes, I have seen one under Bill's arm when he came out of school. It's a Book. That's it. A BOOK!

"Come to think of it, just the other day I heard Mr. Pumpkin telling Bill that Books are very precious. 'He who owns Books and loves them is wise.' That is what he said.

"He who owns Books and loves them is wise," repeated Petunia to herself. And she thought as hard and as long as she could. "Well, then," she said at last, "if I take this Book with me, and love it, I will be wise too. And no one will call me a silly goose ever again."

So Petunia picked up the Book, and off she went with it.

She slept with it . . .

she swam with it.

And, knowing that she was so wise, Petunia also became proud,

and prouder   and prouder . . .   so proud

that her neck stretched out several notches.

It was King, the rooster, who first noticed the change in Petunia. He said, "Maybe Petunia is not so silly after all. She has a Book. And she looks so wise that she must be so."

And the other animals began to believe in Petunia's wisdom too. They asked her for advice and opinions, and Petunia was glad to help—even when she was not asked.

Petunia grew still prouder and her neck stretched out *another* notch.

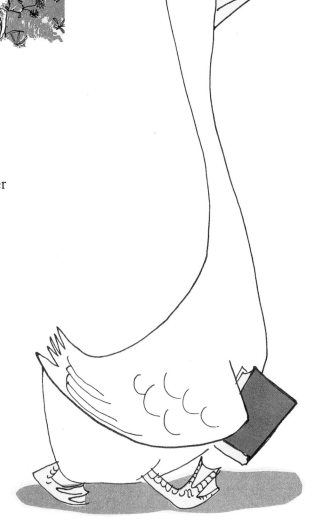

At the chicken coop, Ida, the hen, was cackling excitedly among her chicks. "Oh, Petunia," she said, "my chicks and I have been for a walk in the woods, and I think I've lost some of them. The farmer says I had nine, but I can't count so very well. Please, wise Petunia, count my chicks to see if they're all here."

"Glad to help," said Petunia. "Hmm. Let's see. Three chicks at the fountain. Three at the feeder. Three about your legs. Now—three times three? That makes six. . . ."

"Six?" asked Ida. "Six! Is that less than nine?"

"That's *more* than nine, not less," said Petunia. "*Lots* more, my dear!"

"*More than nine?* Good gracious! As if I hadn't enough worries with my own nine chicks. And where do those other chicks come from? Oh dear, I'll never be happy again."

Poor worried Ida.

But Petunia had other things to do.

Beside the hedgerow she met Straw, the horse, who was in pain from a toothache.

"Petunia," groaned Straw, "I'm dying. Surely, with your wisdom, you can stop this horrible pain."

"Glad to help," said Petunia. "Open your mouth, Why . . . you poor Straw . . . all these teeth! No wonder you have a toothache.

"Look at me. Do I have teeth? Of course not. So I have no toothache. I am going to stop that pain right now. I am going to pull *all* those teeth out. *All* of them. Let me get some pliers. . . ."

But Straw would not wait for the pliers. He was so afraid to lose his teeth that he never talked of his toothache to another soul. He suffered in silence.

Poor forlorn horse.

But Petunia had other things to do.

Cotton, the kitten, went up the tree but could not come down. While he miaowed and miaowed, his friends called for Petunia.

"Glad to help," said Petunia. "I know just what to do. Since none of you is tall enough to reach Cotton, all of you will do it together. Donkey on top of Clover, Pig on top of Donkey, and so on up. Simple."

So Donkey climbed on top of Clover;
Pig on top of Donkey;
Goat on top of Pig;
Sheep on top of Goat;
Piggy on top of Sheep;
Turkey on top of Piggy;
Duck on top of Turkey;
Hen on top of Duck. . . .
Suddenly Clover cried out,
 "Stop! My legs feel wobbly."
And she sat . . .

. . . and Donkey and the rest
fell into a heap, and
Cotton was so scared that
he fell on top of them.
They were all full of bumps.

"Well," said Petunia, "Cotton
is *down*."

So he was, poor bruised kitten.

But Petunia had other things to
do. Getting prouder all the time,
she felt her neck stretch further out.

She now wandered down the meadow, where she found some other friends gathered around a box.

"Ah, wise Petunia!" they shouted. "We found this box in the ditch beside the road. Maybe it's food, Petunia. Please tell us what the writing on it says."

"Glad to help," said Petunia. "Now, let's see . . . Why, CANDIES. That's what it says on that box. Yes, candies. You may eat them. Yes, of course."

No sooner had Petunia given the word than seven greedy mouths tore up the box and grabbed the candies out of it, and . . .

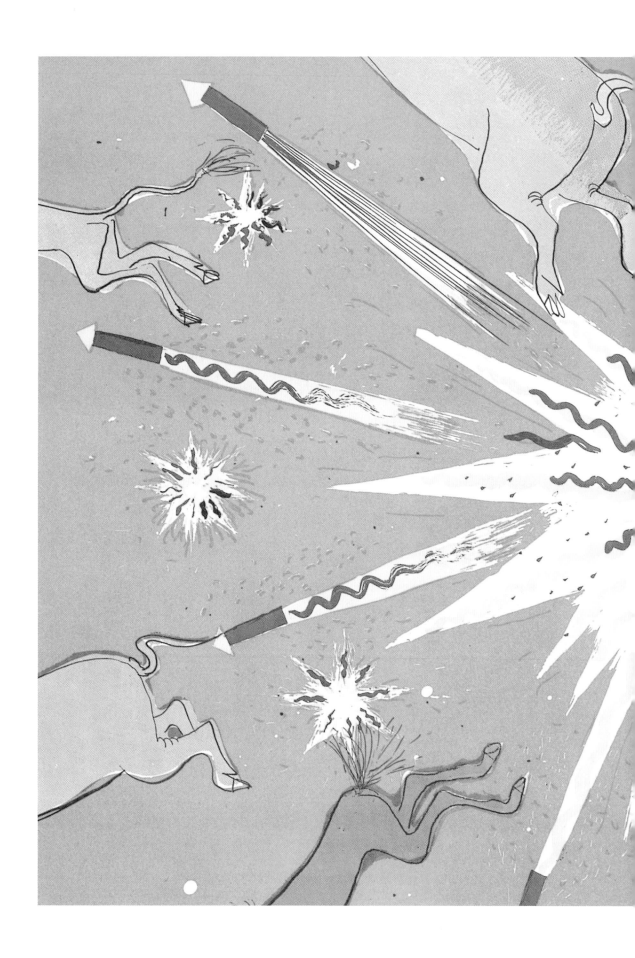

What a sight the animals were!
Some were burned.

Some were bruised.

Straw still suffered in silence.

Ida still worried about her chicks.

All the barnyard was in trouble, and all because of Petunia.

Petunia's pride and wisdom had exploded with the firecrackers. Her neck had shrunk back to its old size and was all bandaged up. She was the most downhearted of all, for she saw now that she was not a bit wise.

But suddenly Petunia spied the Book. The firecrackers had blown it open so that the pages showed. She had never seen them before. Now she saw that there was something written inside the Book which she could not read. So she sat down and thought and thought and thought, until at last she sighed, "Now I understand. It was not enough to carry wisdom under my wing. I must put it in my mind and in my heart. And to do that I must learn to read."

Petunia was filled with joy. At once she began to work so that one day she could be truly wise. Then she would help make her friends happy.

First Tomato

Written and illustrated by Rosemary Wells

Originally published in 1992

Claire ate only three spoons
of cornflakes for breakfast.

On the way to school
her shoes filled with snow.

By eleven in the morning,
math had been going on for two hours.

Lunch was Claire's least favorite—
baloney sandwiches.

At playtime Claire was the only girl not able to do a cartwheel.

Once again the bus was late. Claire needs a visit to the Bunny Planet.

Far beyond the moon and stars,
Twenty light-years south of Mars,

Spins the gentle Bunny Planet
And the Bunny Queen is Janet.

Janet says to Claire, "Come in. Here's the day that should have been."

I hear my mother calling
when the summer wind blows,
"Go out in the garden
in your old, old clothes.

Pick me some runner beans
and sugar snap peas.
Find a ripe tomato
and bring it to me, please."

A ruby red tomato is hanging on the vine.
If my mother didn't want it, the tomato would be mine.

It smells of rain and steamy earth
and hot June sun.
In the whole tomato garden
it's the only ripe one.
I close my eyes and breathe in
its fat, red smell.
I wish that I could eat it now
and never, never tell.

But I save it for my mother
without another look.

I wash the beans and shell the peas and watch my mother cook.

I hear my mother calling
when the summer winds blow,

"I've made you First Tomato soup
because I love you so."

Claire's big warm bus comes at last.
Out her window Claire sees the Bunny Planet
near the evening star in the snowy sky.
"It was there all along!" says Claire.

AMELIA BEDELIA

Written by Peggy Parish
Illustrated by Fritz Siebel

Originally published in 1963

"Oh, Amelia Bedelia, your first day of work, and I can't be here. But I made a list for you. You do just what the list says," said Mrs. Rogers.

Mrs. Rogers got into the car with Mr. Rogers.

They drove away.

"My, what nice folks. I'm going to like working here," said Amelia Bedelia.

Amelia Bedelia went inside. "Such a grand house. These must be rich folks. But I must get to work. Here I stand just looking. And me with a whole list of things to do."

Amelia Bedelia stood there a minute longer. "I think I'll make a surprise for them. I'll make lemon-meringue pie. I do make good pies."

So Amelia Bedelia went into the kitchen. She put a little of this and a pinch of that into a bowl. She mixed and she rolled. Soon her pie was ready to go into the oven.

 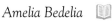

"There," said Amelia Bedelia. "That's done.

"Now let's see what this list says."
Amelia Bedelia read,
Change the towels in the green bathroom.
Amelia Bedelia found the green bathroom. "Those towels are very nice. Why change them?" she thought.

Then Amelia Bedelia remembered what Mrs. Rogers had said. She must do just what the list told her. "Well, all right," said Amelia Bedelia.

Amelia Bedelia got some scissors. She snipped a little here and a little there. And she changed those towels.

"There," said Amelia Bedelia. She looked at the list again.

Dust the furniture.

"Did you ever hear tell of such a silly thing. At my house we undust the furniture. But to each his own way."

Amelia Bedelia took one last look at the bathroom. She saw a big box with the words *Dusting Powder* on it. "Well, look at that. A special powder to dust with!" exclaimed Amelia Bedelia.

So Amelia Bedelia dusted the furniture. "That should be dusty enough. My, how nice it smells."

Draw the drapes when the sun comes in, read Amelia Bedelia. She looked up. The sun was coming in.

Amelia Bedelia looked at the list again. "Draw the drapes? That's what it says. I'm not much of a hand at drawing, but I'll try."

So Amelia Bedelia sat right down and she drew those drapes.

Amelia Bedelia marked off about the drapes.

"Now what?"

Put the lights out when you finish in the living room.

Amelia Bedelia thought about this a minute. She switched off the lights. Then she carefully unscrewed each bulb.

And Amelia Bedelia put the lights out. "So those things need to be aired out, too. Just like pillows and babies. Oh, I do have a lot to learn."

"My pie!" exclaimed Amelia Bedelia. She hurried to the kitchen.

"Just right," she said. She took the pie out of the oven and put it on the table to cool. Then she looked at the list.

The meat market will deliver a steak and a chicken.

Please trim the fat before you put the steak in the icebox.

And please dress the chicken.

When the meat arrived, Amelia Bedelia opened the bag. She looked at the steak for a long time. "Yes," she said. "That will do nicely."

Amelia Bedelia got some lace and bits of ribbon. And Amelia Bedelia trimmed that fat before she put the steak in the icebox.

"Now I must dress the chicken. I wonder if she wants a he chicken or a she chicken?" said Amelia Bedelia.

Amelia Bedelia went right to work. Soon the chicken was finished.

Amelia Bedelia heard the door open. "The folks are back," she said. She rushed out to meet them.

"Amelia Bedelia, why are all the light bulbs outside?" asked Mr. Rogers.

"The list just said to put the lights out," said Amelia Bedelia. "It didn't say to bring them back in. Oh, I do hope they didn't get aired too long."

"Amelia Bedelia, the sun will fade the furniture. I asked you to draw the drapes," said Mrs. Rogers.

"I did! I did! See," said Amelia Bedelia. She held up her picture.

Then Mrs. Rogers saw the furniture. "The furniture!" she cried.

"Did I dust it well enough?" asked Amelia Bedelia. "That's such nice dusting powder."

Mr. Rogers went to wash his hands. "I say," he called. "These are very unusual towels."

Mrs. Rogers dashed into the bathroom. "Oh, my best towels," she said.

"Didn't I change them enough?" asked Amelia Bedelia.

"Was the meat delivered?" asked Mrs. Rogers.

"Yes," said Amelia Bedelia. "I trimmed the fat just like you said. It does look nice."

Mrs. Rogers rushed to the icebox. She opened it.

"Lace! Ribbons! Oh, dear!" said Mrs. Rogers.

"The chicken—you dressed the chicken?" asked Mrs. Rogers.

"Yes, and I found the nicest box to put him in," said Amelia Bedelia.

"Box!" exclaimed Mrs. Rogers.

Mrs. Rogers hurried over to the box. She lifted the lid. There lay the chicken. And he was just as dressed as he could be.

Mrs. Rogers was angry. She was very angry. She opened her mouth. Mrs. Rogers meant to tell Amelia Bedelia she was fired. But before she could get the words out, Mr. Rogers put something in her mouth. It was so good Mrs. Rogers forgot about being angry. "Lemon-meringue pie!" she exclaimed.

"I made it to surprise you," said Amelia Bedelia happily.

So right then and there Mr. and Mrs. Rogers decided that Amelia Bedelia must stay. And so she did.

Mrs. Rogers learned to say undust the furniture, unlight the lights, close the drapes, and things like that.

Mr. Rogers didn't care if Amelia Bedelia trimmed all of his steaks with lace.

All he cared about was having her there to make lemon-meringue pie.

I Am a Bunny

Written by Ole Risom
Illustrated by Richard Scarry

Originally published in 1963

I am a bunny.
My name is Nicholas.
I live in a hollow tree.

In the spring, I like to pick flowers.

I chase the butterflies, and the butterflies chase me.

In the summer, I like to lie in the sun and watch the birds.

And I like to
watch the frogs
in the pond.

When it rains, I keep dry under a toadstool.

I blow the dandelion seeds into the air.

In the fall, I like to watch the leaves falling from the trees.

I watch the animals
getting ready for the winter.

 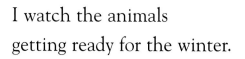

And, when the winter comes,
I watch the snow falling from the sky.

Then I curl up in my hollow tree
and dream about spring.

HARRY THE DIRTY DOG

Written by Gene Zion
Illustrated by Margaret Bloy Graham

Originally published in 1956

Harry was a white dog with black spots
who liked everything
except . . . getting a bath.
So one day when he heard the water
running in the tub,
he took the scrubbing brush . . .

and buried it in the back yard.

Then he ran away from home.

He played where they were fixing the street and got very dirty.

He played at the railroad and got even dirtier.

He played tag with other dogs and became dirtier still.

He slid down a coal chute and got the dirtiest of all.
In fact, he changed from a white dog with black spots,
to a black dog with white spots.

Although there were many other things to do,
Harry began to wonder if his family thought
that he had *really* run away.

He felt tired and hungry too,
so without stopping on the way
he ran back home.

When Harry got to his house,
he crawled through the fence
and sat looking at the back door.

One of the family looked out and said,
"There's a strange dog in the back yard . . .
by the way, has anyone seen Harry?"

When Harry heard this, he tried very hard
to show them *he* was Harry. He started to do
all his old, clever tricks. He flip-flopped

and he flop-flipped.
He rolled over
and played dead.

He danced and he sang.

He did these tricks over and over again,
but everyone shook his head and said,
"Oh, no, it couldn't be Harry."

Harry gave up
and walked slowly toward the gate,
but suddenly he stopped.

He ran to a corner of the garden
and started to dig furiously.
Soon he jumped away from the hole
barking short, happy barks.

He'd found the scrubbing brush!
And carrying it in his mouth,
he ran into the house.

Up the stairs he dashed,
with the family
following close behind.

He jumped into the bathtub and sat up begging,
with the scrubbing brush in his mouth,
a trick he certainly had never done before.

"This little doggie wants a bath!"
cried the little girl, and her father said,
"Why don't you and your brother give him one?"

Harry's bath was the soapiest one he'd ever had.
It worked like magic. As soon as the children
started to scrub, they began shouting,
"Mummy! Daddy! Look, look! Come quick!"

"It's Harry! It's Harry! It's Harry!" they cried.
Harry wagged his tail and was very, very happy.
His family combed and brushed him lovingly, and
he became once again a white dog with black spots.

It was wonderful to be home.
After dinner, Harry fell asleep
in his favorite place, happily dreaming
of how much fun it had been getting dirty.
He slept so soundly,
he didn't even feel the scrubbing brush
he'd hidden under his pillow.

WHOSE MOUSE ARE YOU?

Written by Robert Kraus
Illustrated by Jose Aruego

Originally published in 1970

Whose mouse are you?

Nobody's mouse.

Where is your mother?

Inside the cat.

Where is your father?

Caught in a trap.

Where is your sister?

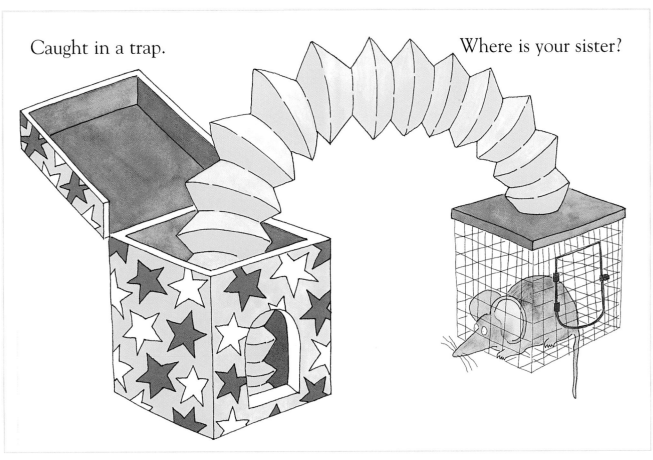

Far from home.

Where is your brother?

I have none.   What will you do?

Shake my mother out of the cat!

Free my father from the trap!

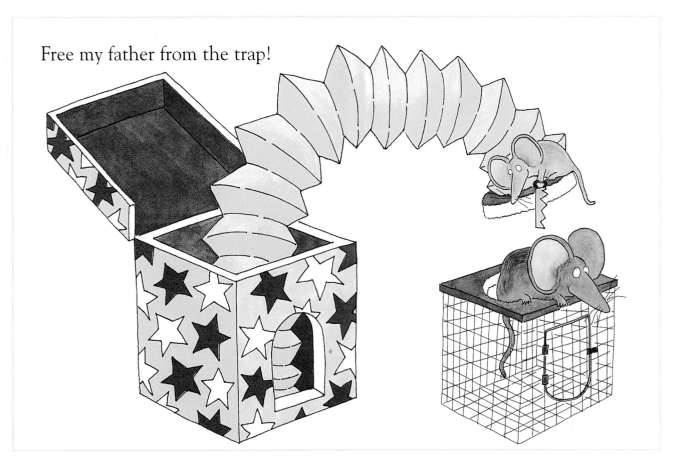

Find my sister and bring her home.

Wish for a brother as I have none. Now whose mouse are you?

My mother's mouse, she loves me so.

My father's mouse, from head to toe.

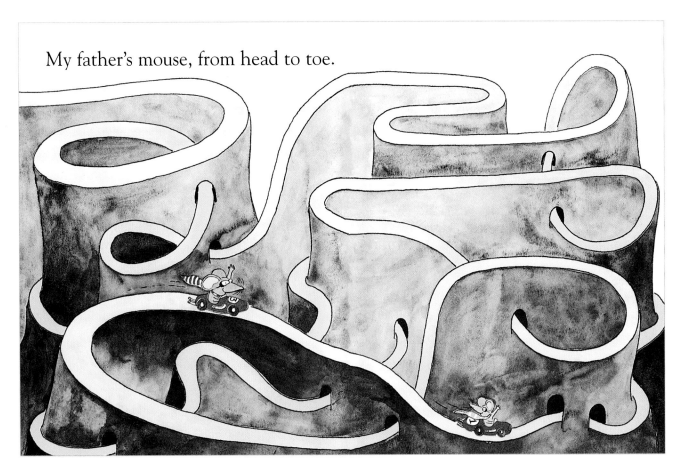

My sister's mouse, she loves me too.

My brother's mouse....   Your brother's mouse?

My brother's mouse—he's *brand* new!

OWEN

Written and illustrated by Kevin Henkes

Originally published in 1993

Owen had a fuzzy yellow blanket.
He'd had it since he was a baby.
He loved it with all his heart.

"Fuzzy goes where I go," said Owen.
And Fuzzy did.
Upstairs, downstairs, in-between.
Inside, outside, upside down.

"Fuzzy likes what I like," said Owen.
And Fuzzy did.
Orange juice, grape juice, chocolate milk.
Ice cream, peanut butter, applesauce cake.

"Isn't he getting a little old to be carrying that thing around?" asked Mrs. Tweezers. "Haven't you heard of the Blanket Fairy?"

Owen's parents hadn't.

Mrs. Tweezers filled them in.

That night Owen's parents told Owen to put Fuzzy under his pillow. In the morning Fuzzy would be gone, but the Blanket Fairy would leave an absolutely wonderful, positively perfect, especially terrific big-boy gift in its place.

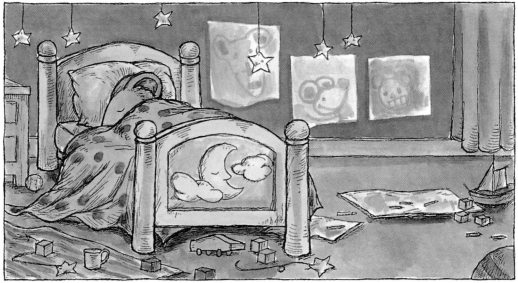

Owen stuffed Fuzzy inside his pajama pants and went to sleep.

"No Blanket Fairy," said Owen in the morning.

"No kidding," said Owen's mother.

"No wonder," said Owen's father.

"Fuzzy's dirty," said Owen's mother.

"Fuzzy's torn and ratty," said Owen's father.

"No," said Owen. "Fuzzy is perfect."

And Fuzzy was.

Fuzzy played Captain Plunger with Owen.

Fuzzy helped Owen become invisible.

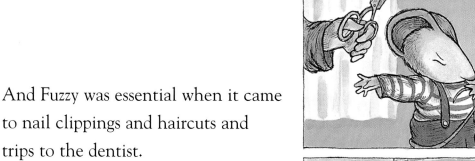

And Fuzzy was essential when it came to nail clippings and haircuts and trips to the dentist.

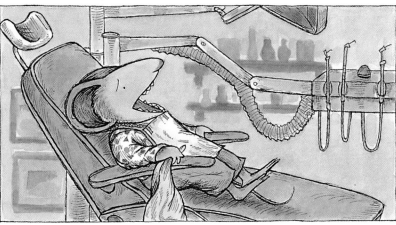

"Can't be a baby forever," said Mrs. Tweezers. "Haven't you heard of the vinegar trick?"
Owen's parents hadn't.
Mrs. Tweezers filled them in.

When Owen wasn't looking, his father dipped Owen's
favorite corner of Fuzzy into a jar of vinegar.

Owen sniffed it and smelled it and sniffed it.
He picked a new favorite corner.

Then he rubbed the smelly corner all
around his sandbox, buried it in the
garden, and dug it up again.
"Good as new," said Owen.

Fuzzy wasn't very fuzzy anymore.
But Owen didn't mind.

He carried it.
And wore it.
And dragged it.

He sucked it.
And hugged it.
And twisted it.

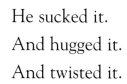

"What are we going to do?" asked Owen's mother.

"School is starting soon," said Owen's father.

"Can't bring a blanket to school," said Mrs. Tweezers.

"Haven't you heard of saying no?" Owen's parents hadn't.

Mrs. Tweezers filled them in.

"I *have* to bring Fuzzy to school," said Owen.

"No," said Owen's mother.

"No," said Owen's father.

Owen buried his face in Fuzzy.

He started to cry and would not stop.

"Don't worry," said Owen's mother.

"It'll be all right," said Owen's father.

And then suddenly Owen's mother said, "I have an idea!"

It was an absolutely wonderful, positively perfect, especially terrific idea.

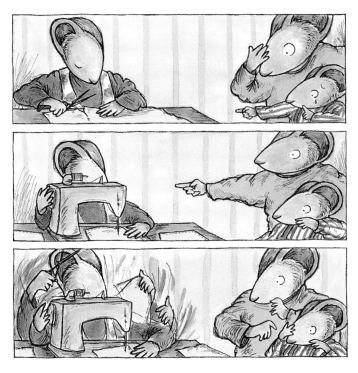

First she snipped.

And then she sewed.

Then she snipped again and sewed some more.

Snip, snip, snip.

Sew, sew, sew.

"Dry your eyes."

"Wipe your nose."

Hooray, hooray, hooray!

Now Owen carries one of his not-so-fuzzy handkerchiefs with him wherever he goes....

And Mrs. Tweezers doesn't say a thing.

THE STORY OF FERDINAND

Written by Munro Leaf
Illustrated by Robert Lawson

Originally published in 1936

Once upon a time in Spain there was a little bull and his name was Ferdinand.

All the other little bulls he lived with would run and jump and butt their heads together, but not Ferdinand.

He liked to sit just quietly and smell the flowers.

He had a favorite spot out in the pasture under a cork tree.

It was his favorite tree and he would sit in its shade all day and smell the flowers.

Sometimes his mother, who was a cow, would worry about him. She was afraid he would be lonesome all by himself.

"Why don't you run and play with the other little bulls and skip and butt your head?" she would say.

But Ferdinand would shake his head. "I like it better here where I can sit just quietly and smell the flowers."

His mother saw that he was not lonesome, and because she was an understanding mother, even though she was a cow, she let him just sit there and be happy.

As the years went by Ferdinand grew and grew until he was very big and strong.

All the other bulls who had grown up with him in the same pasture would fight each other all day. They would butt each other and stick each other with their horns. What they wanted most of all was to be picked to fight at the bull fights in Madrid.

But not Ferdinand—he still liked to sit just quietly under the cork tree and smell the flowers.

One day five men came in very funny hats to pick the biggest, fastest, roughest bull to fight in the bull fights in Madrid.

All the other bulls ran around snorting and butting, leaping and jumping so the men would think that they were very very strong and fierce and pick them.

Ferdinand knew that they wouldn't pick him and he didn't care. So he went out to his favorite cork tree to sit down.

He didn't look where he was sitting and instead of sitting on the nice cool grass in the shade he sat on a bumble bee.

Well, if you were a bumble bee and a bull sat on you what would you do? You would sting him. And that is just what this bee did to Ferdinand.

Wow! Did it hurt! Ferdinand jumped up with a snort. He ran around puffing and snorting, butting and pawing the ground as if he were crazy.

The five men saw him and they all shouted with joy. Here was the largest and fiercest bull of all. Just the one for the bull fights in Madrid!

So they took him away for the bull fight day in a cart.

What a day it was! Flags were flying, bands were playing…and all the lovely ladies had flowers in their hair.

They had a parade into the bull ring.

First came the Banderilleros with long sharp pins with ribbons on them to stick in the bull and make him mad.

Next came the Picadores who rode skinny horses and they had

long spears to stick in the bull and make him madder.

Then came the Matador, the proudest of all—he thought he was very handsome, and bowed to the ladies. He had a red cape and a sword and was supposed to stick the bull last of all.

Then came the bull, and you know who that was, don't you?

—FERDINAND.

They called him Ferdinand the Fierce and all the Banderilleros were afraid of him and the Picadores were afraid of him and the Matador was scared stiff.

Ferdinand ran to the middle of the ring and everyone shouted and clapped because they thought he was going to fight fiercely and butt and snort and stick his horns around.

But not Ferdinand. When he got to the middle of the ring he saw the flowers in all the lovely ladies' hair and he just sat down quietly and smelled.

He wouldn't fight and be fierce no matter what they did. He just sat and smelled. And the Banderilleros were mad and the Picadores were madder and the Matador was so mad he cried because he couldn't show off with his cape and sword.

So they had to take Ferdinand home.

And for all I know his is sitting there still, under his favorite cork tree, smelling the flowers just quietly.

He is very happy.

THE SNEETCHES

(from THE SNEETCHES AND OTHER STORIES)

Written and illustrated by Dr. Seuss

Originally published in 1961

Now, the Star-Belly Sneetches
Had bellies with stars.
The Plain-Belly Sneetches
Had none upon thars.

Those stars weren't so big. They were really so small
You might think such a thing wouldn't matter at all.

But, because they had stars, all the Star-Belly Sneetches
Would brag, "We're the best kind of Sneetch on the beaches."
With their snoots in the air, they would sniff and they'd snort
"We'll have nothing to do with the Plain-Belly sort!"
And whenever they met some, when they were out walking,
They'd hike right on past them without even talking.

When the Star-Belly children went out to play ball,
Could a Plain Belly get in the game . . . ? Not at all.
You only could play if your bellies had stars
And the Plain-Belly children had none upon thars.

When the Star-Belly Sneetches had frankfurter roasts
Or picnics or parties or marshmallow toasts,
They never invited the Plain-Belly Sneetches.
They left them out cold, in the dark of the beaches.
They kept them away. Never let them come near.
And that's how they treated them year after year.

Then ONE day, it seems . . . while the Plain-Belly Sneetches
Were moping and doping alone on the beaches,
Just sitting there wishing their bellies had stars . . .
A stranger zipped up in the strangest of cars!

"My friends," he announced in a voice clear and keen,
"My name is Sylvester McMonkey McBean.
And I've heard of your troubles. I've heard you're unhappy.
But I can fix that. I'm the Fix-it-Up Chappie.
I've come here to help you. I have what you need.
And my prices are low. And I work at great speed.
And my work is one hundred per cent guaranteed!"

Then, quickly, Sylvester McMonkey McBean
Put together a very peculiar machine.
And he said, "You want stars like a Star-Belly Sneetch . . . ?
My friends, you can have them for three dollars each!"

"Just pay me your money and hop right aboard!"
So they clambered inside. Then the big machine roared
And it klonked. And it bonked. And it jerked. And it berked
And it bopped them about. But the thing really worked!
When the Plain-Belly Sneetches popped out, they had stars!
They actually did. They had stars upon thars!

288

Then they yelled at the ones who had stars from the start,
"We're exactly like you! You can't tell us apart.
We're all just the same, now, you snooty old smarties!
And now we can go to your frankfurter parties."

"Good grief!" groaned the ones who had stars at the first.
"We're *still* the best Sneetches and they are the worst.
But, now, how in the world will we know," they all frowned,
"If which kind is what, or the other way round?"

Then up came McBean with a very sly wink
And he said, "Things are not quite as bad as you think.
So you don't know who's who. That is perfectly true.
But come with me, friends. Do you know what I'll do?
I'll make you, again, the best Sneetches on beaches
And all it will cost you is ten dollars eaches."

"Belly stars are no longer in style," said McBean.
"What you need is a trip through my Star-*Off* Machine.
This wondrous contraption will take *off* your stars
So you won't look like Sneetches who have them on thars."
And that handy machine
Working very precisely
Removed all the stars from their tummies quite nicely.

Then, with snoots in the air, they paraded about
And they opened their beaks and they let out a shout,
"We know who is who! Now there isn't a doubt.
The best kind of Sneetches are Sneetches without!"

Then, of course, those with stars all got frightfully mad.
To be wearing a star now was frightfully bad.
Then, of course, old Sylvester McMonkey McBean
Invited *them* into his Star-Off Machine.

Then, of course from THEN on, as you probably guess,
Things really got into a horrible mess.

All the rest of that day, on those wild screaming beaches,
The Fix-it-Up Chappie kept fixing up Sneetches.
Off again! On again!
In again! Out again!
Through the machines they raced round and about again,
Changing their stars every minute or two.
They kept paying money. They kept running through
Until neither the Plain nor the Star-Bellies knew
Whether this one was that one…or that one was this one
Or which one was what one…or what one was who.

Then, when every last cent
Of their money was spent,
The Fix-it-Up Chappie packed up
And he went.

And he laughed as he drove
In his car up the beach,
"They never will learn.
No. You can't teach a Sneetch!"

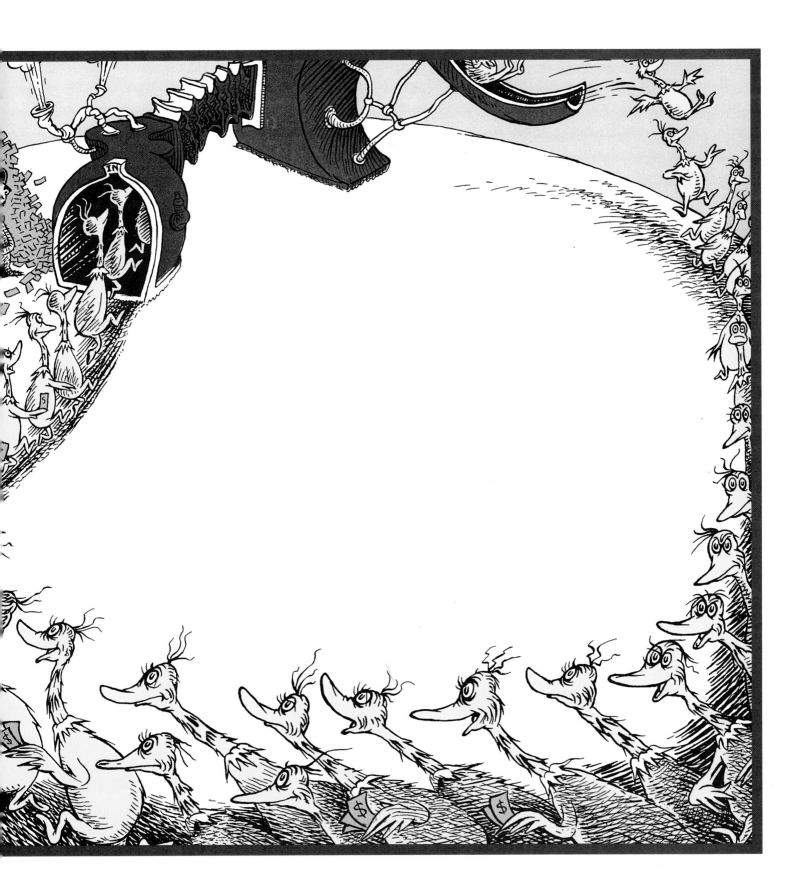

But McBean was quite wrong. I'm quite happy to say
That the Sneetches got really quite smart on that day,
The day they decided that Sneetches are Sneetches
And no kind of Sneetch is the best on the beaches.
That day, all the Sneetches forgot about stars
And whether they had one, or not, upon thars.

THE STORY OF LITTLE BABAJI

Written by Helen Bannerman
Illustrated by Fred Marcellino

Text originally published in 1899
Illustrations originally published in 1996

This story was originally published as *The Story of Little Black Sambo*.
On page vii, the Note to Parents explains its happy transformation in 1996 into
The Story of Little Babaji, a presentation that is more in tune with social mores today.

Once upon a time there was a little boy,
and his name was Little Babaji.

And his Mother was called Mamaji.

And his Father was called Papaji.

And Mamaji made him a beautiful little Red
Coat, and a pair of beautiful little Blue Trousers.

And Papaji went to the Bazaar,
and bought him a beautiful Green
Umbrella, and a lovely little Pair
of Purple Shoes with Crimson
Soles and Crimson Linings.

And then wasn't Little
Babaji grand?

So he put on all his Fine Clothes, and went out for a walk in the Jungle.

And by and by he met a Tiger. And the Tiger said to him, "Little Babaji, I'm going to eat you up!"

And Little Babaji said, "Oh! Please Mr. Tiger, don't eat me up, and I'll give you my beautiful little Red Coat." So the Tiger said, "Very well, I won't eat you this time, but you must give me your beautiful little Red Coat."

So the Tiger got poor Little Babaji's beautiful little Red Coat, and went away saying, "Now I'm the grandest Tiger in the Jungle."

And Little Babaji went on, and by and by he met another Tiger, and it said to him, "Little Babaji, I'm going to eat you up!" And Little Babaji said, "Oh! Please Mr. Tiger, don't eat me up, and I'll give you my beautiful little Blue Trousers." So the Tiger said, "Very well, I won't eat you this time, but you must give me your beautiful little Blue Trousers."

So the Tiger got poor Little Babaji's beautiful little Blue Trousers, and went away saying, "Now *I'm* the grandest Tiger in the Jungle."

And Little Babaji went on, and by and by he met another Tiger, and it said to him, "Little Babaji, I'm going to eat you up!" And Little Babaji said, "Oh! Please Mr. Tiger, don't eat me up, and I'll give you my beautiful little Purple Shoes with Crimson Soles and Crimson Linings."

But the Tiger said, "What use would your shoes be to me? I've got four feet, and you've got only two. You haven't got enough shoes for me."

But Little Babaji said, "You could wear them on your ears."

"So I could," said the Tiger, "that's a very good idea. Give them to me, and I won't eat you this time."

So the Tiger got poor Little Babaji's beautiful little Purple Shoes with Crimson Soles and Crimson Linings, and went away saying, "Now *I'm* the grandest Tiger in the Jungle."

And by and by Little Babaji met another Tiger, and it said to him, "Little Babaji, I'm going to eat you up!" And Little Babaji said, "Oh! Please Mr. Tiger, don't eat me up, and I'll give you my beautiful Green Umbrella." But the Tiger said, "How can I carry an umbrella, when I need all my paws for walking with?"

"You could tie a knot on your tail and carry it that way," said Little Babaji. "So I could," said the Tiger. "Give it to me, and I won't eat you this time."

So he got poor Little Babaji's beautiful Green Umbrella, and went away saying, "Now *I'm* the grandest Tiger in the Jungle."

And poor Little Babaji went away crying, because the cruel Tigers had taken all his fine clothes.

Presently he heard a horrible noise that sounded like "Gr–r–r–r–r–rrrrrrr," and it got louder and louder. "Oh! dear!" said Little Babaji, "there are all the Tigers coming back to eat me up! What shall I do?" So he ran quickly to a palm tree, and peeped round it to see what the matter was.

And there he saw all the Tigers fighting, and disputing which of them was the grandest.

The Story of Little Babaji   295

And at last they all got so angry that they jumped up and took off all the fine clothes, and began to tear each other with their claws, and bite each other with their great big white teeth.

And they came rolling and tumbling right to the foot of the very tree where Little Babaji was hiding, but he jumped quickly in behind the umbrella. And the Tigers all caught hold of each other's tails, as they wrangled and scrambled, and so they found themselves in a ring round the tree.

Then, when the Tigers were very wee and very far away, Little Babaji jumped up, and called out, "Oh! Tigers! why have you taken off all your nice clothes? Don't you want them any more?" But the Tigers only answered, "Gr–r–rrrrr!"

Then Little Babaji said, "If you want them, say so, or I'll take them away." But the Tigers would not let go of each other's tails, and so they could only say "Gr–r–r–r–rrrrrrr!"

So Little Babaji put on all his fine clothes again and walked off.

And the Tigers were very, very angry, but still they would not let go of each other's tails.

And they were so angry that they ran round the tree, trying to eat each other up, and they ran faster and faster . . .

296

till they were whirling round so fast that you couldn't see their legs at all. And they still ran faster and faster and faster . . .

till they all just melted away, and there was nothing left but a great big pool of melted butter (or "ghi," as it is called in India) round the foot of the tree.

Now Papaji was just coming home from his work, with a great big brass pot in his arms, and when he saw what was left of all the Tigers he said, "Oh! what lovely melted butter! I'll take that home to Mamaji for her to cook with." So he put it all into the great big brass pot, and took it home to Mamaji to cook with.

When Mamaji saw the melted butter, wasn't she pleased! "Now," said she, "we'll all have pancakes for supper!"

So she got flour and eggs and milk and sugar and butter, and she made a huge big plate of the most lovely pancakes. And she fried them in the melted butter which the Tigers had made, and they were just as yellow and brown as little Tigers.

And then they all sat down to supper.

And Mamaji ate Twenty-seven pancakes, and Papaji ate Fifty-five.

But Little Babaji ate a Hundred and Sixty-nine, because he was so hungry.

BIOGRAPHICAL NOTES

AIKEN, JOAN [p. 198, British, b. 1924], the daughter of American poet Conrad Aiken, is the author of dozens of award-winning novels for children, poems, picture books, plays, retellings of folk tales, and short stories, such as "The Elves in the Shelves," which appears in this collection. Aiken's best-known work, *The Wolves of Willoughby Chase* (1962), was the first novel in a series of wonderful historical fantasies.

ALLARD, HARRY [p. 99, American, b. 1928] worked for many years as a professor of French before writing his first children's book, *The Stupids Step Out* (1974), illustrated by James Marshall. The pair also created three books about a feared but loved teacher: *Miss Nelson Is Missing!* (1977), *Miss Nelson Is Back* (1982), and *Miss Nelson Has a Field Day* (1985).

ARCHAMBAULT, JOHN [p. 15, American, b. ?] is a poet, journalist, and storyteller who has collaborated with author Bill Martin, Jr., on nine popular children's books, including *Chicka Chicka Boom Boom* (1989), illustrated by Lois Ehlert, and *The Ghost-Eye Tree* (1985). Archambault has also written books of his own, including the picture book *I Love the Mountains: A Traditional Song* (1998).

ARUEGO, JOSE [p. 257, Filipino-born American, b. 1932] has illustrated many humorous books for toddlers and preschoolers, most often with his former wife, the illustrator Ariane Dewey. Both alone and with Dewey, he has frequently collaborated on books written by Robert Kraus, including *Whose Mouse Are You?* (1970), *Leo the Late Bloomer* (1971), and *Herman the Helper* (1974).

AVERILL, ESTHER [p. 119, American, 1902–1992] lived from 1925 to 1935 in Paris where she established the Domino Press, a small publisher of beautiful children's books. It is, however, her stories about the shy little black cat with the red scarf, Jenny Linsky, for which she is remembered. Jenny and all her friends in the Cat Club were based on Averill's own cat and the neighborhood cats that used to gather in a courtyard behind Averill's Greenwich Village home.

BANG, MOLLY [p. 203, American, b. 1943] a storyteller who also illustrates her books, draws on the legends and folk tales of many cultures, as in *The Paper Crane* (1988). Two of her books, *The Grey Lady and the Strawberry Snatcher* (1980) and *Ten, Nine, Eight* (1983), were named Caldecott Honor Books. The latter was inspired by Bang's adopted Bengali daughter and by Bang's conviction that there were not enough books in this country featuring minority children.

BANNERMAN, HELEN [p. 293, Scottish, 1863(?)–1946] lived in India for thirty years and wrote *The Story of Little Black Sambo* (1899) for her two young daughters, who had been left in Scotland for their early education. See page 293 and the Note to Parents for more about this book.

BEMELMANS, LUDWIG [p. 1, Austrian-born American, 1898–1962] considered himself first and foremost a painter, yet he lives on through his books about the fearless Madeline. Inspired by a child who had her appendix taken out in a hospital in France, Bemelmans wrote *Madeline*, a Caldecott Honor Book, in 1938. Five more stories about the adventurous heroine followed, including *Madeline's Rescue* (1953), which won the Caldecott Medal. He wrote and illustrated more than fifteen books for children and wrote more than twenty for adults.

BERENSTAIN, STAN and JAN [p. 191, both American, both b. 1923] launched their Bear family in 1962 with *The Big Honey Hunt*. The Bears—Mama, Papa, Sister, and Brother—now appear in well over 100 books and are one of the most beloved storybook families of the last quarter century. Unlike most of the Berenstain Bear books since 1981, which deal with behavioral issues and are for slightly older children, *The Berenstain Bears and the Spooky Old Tree* (1978) explores spatial concepts and is great fun to read to a very young child.

BROWN, MARC [p. 214, American, b. 1946] is the creator of the appealing young aardvark named Arthur, who wears glasses and has a pesky little sister named D.W. Arthur's adventures began in 1976 with the picture book *Arthur's Nose* and now include, in addition to more than thirty books, an award-winning daily television show. The enormous popularity of Arthur lies in Brown's knack of portraying real growing-up experiences with humor and lively illustrations. In addition to his Arthur books, which he both writes and illustrates, he has illustrated many notable books, ranging from the useful *Dinosaurs, Beware! A Safety Guide* (1982), by his wife Laurie Krasny Brown, to *Read-Aloud Rhymes for the Very Young* (1986), selected by Jack Prelutsky.

BROWN, MARGARET WISE [p. 34, American, 1910–1952] wrote more than 100 books for children in her short but remarkable career. The author of the classics *Goodnight Moon* (1947) and *The Runaway Bunny* (1942), she was also a vital force in revolutionizing children's literature for the under-six set. Inspired by her mentor, Bank Street College of Education founder Lucy Sprague Mitchell, Brown was one of the first authors to write books that presented real experiences of modern children.

BURTON, VIRGINIA LEE [p. 139, American, 1909–1968] wonderfully anthropomorphized common machines such as Choo Choo, the runaway engine, Mary Anne, Mike Mulligan's steam shovel, and Katy, the brave snowplow, which have each earned a place in the hearts of generations of children. A true perfectionist who would redraw picture after picture until she got them "just right," Burton earned the Caldecott Medal for *The Little House* (1942).

CANNON, JANELL [p. 208, American, b. 1957] worked for many years at a public library, where she created award-winning summer reading programs. A self-taught artist and writer, she wrote and illustrated *Stellaluna* (1993) in hopes of debunking negative myths about bats, one of the many unusual animals she loves. Her other books include *Trupp: A Fuzzhead Tale* (1995) and *Verdi* (1997).

CONRAD, PAM [p. 155, American, 1947–1996], widely known for her critically acclaimed historical novel *Prairie Songs* (1985), also wrote many works of fiction for older children, along with picture books and stories for young readers. Conrad's characters grow through loss, as do the friends and family in *The Tub People* (1989) and the sailor in *The Lost Sailor* (1992), both illustrated by Caldecott Medalist Richard Egielski.

CREWS, DONALD [p. 51, American, b. 1938] is a pioneer in the category of "less-is-more" early-learning concept books, with his spare text and highly graphic art. His works include the Caldecott Honor Books *Freight Train* (1978), an introduction to colors and motion, and *Truck* (1980), a look at shapes and road signs, his counting book *Ten Black Dots* (1968), the very busy *Harbor* (1982), and his view of the child's world in *Parade* (1983) and *School Bus* (1984).

CRUZ, RAY [p. 86, American, b. 1933] has worked in textile and wallpaper design, package design, advertising, and, of course, book illustration, as exemplified by the classic *Alexander and the Terrible, Horrible, No Good, Very Bad Day* (1972) and *Alexander Who Used to Be Rich Last Sunday* (1978), both by Judith Viorst.

DE BRUNHOFF, JEAN [p. 180, French, 1899–1937] will live forever through Babar, the universally loved elephant he created. Inspired by stories his wife made up for their children, de Brunhoff wrote and illustrated *The Story of Babar* (1931), which was quickly followed by six more books about the popular pachyderm. Wonderful oversize volumes with all of the text printed in elegant script, these original Babar books warmly present the positive sides of family life and society at large. De Brunhoff's son, Laurent, has continued to create Babar books in many formats.

DUVOISIN, ROGER [p. 218, Swiss-born American, 1904–1980] wrote and illustrated more than forty books and illustrated over 140 more. He was the creator of the humorous books about Veronica the hippo and Petunia the silly goose, and he illustrated the popular "Happy Lion" series, written by his wife, Louise Fatio. He received the Caldecott Medal for *White Snow, Bright Snow* (1947) by Alvin Tresselt.

EGIELSKI, RICHARD [p. 155, American, b. 1952] won the Caldecott Medal for *Hey, Al* (1986), one of his many collaborations with Arthur Yorinks. Preferring highly personal picture books with provocative and wry texts, Egielski brings the characters in Pam Conrad's *The Tub People* (1989) and *The Tub Grandfather* (1993) to life by magically endowing stiff wooden toys with powerful yet tender personalities.

EHLERT, LOIS [p. 15, American, b. 1934] is the illustrator and author-illustrator of more than a dozen picture books for children. An artist with a sure sense of graphics and design, Ehlert has created many concept books, including *Color Zoo* (1989), a Caldecott Honor Book; *Eating the Alphabet* (1989); *Hands* (1997); and *Chicka Chicka Boom Boom* (1989), written by Bill Martin, Jr., and John Archambault.

GÁG, WANDA [p. 76, American, 1893–1946] captured the imagination of generations of children with her homey black-and-white pictures and delightfully rhythmic texts. *Millions of Cats* (1928), her very first and most famous children's book, won a Newbery Honor Award. Gág received another Newbery Honor for *The ABC Bunny* (1933) and Caldecott Medals for her retelling of *Snow White and the Seven Dwarfs* (1938) and for *Nothing at All* (1941), a story about an invisible dog.

GRAHAM, MARGARET BLOY [p. 249, Canadian-born American, b. 1920] has illustrated over a dozen picture books, most collaborations with her then husband Gene Zion, among them their enduringly entertaining Harry books: *Harry the Dirty Dog* (1956), *No Roses for Harry!* (1958), *Harry and the Lady Next Door* (1960), and *Harry by the Sea* (1965). She is also the illustrator of two Caldecott Honor Books, *All Falling Down* (1951), her first collaboration with Zion, and *The Storm Book* (1952) by Charlotte Zolotow.

HENKES, KEVIN [p. 265, American, b. 1960] has created numerous comforting and satisfying picture books dealing with common family situations, using his expressive and amusing cast of mice-children to bring a resonant, childlike authenticity to his stories. In the Caldecott Honor Book *Owen* (1993), the title character outwits all attempts at separating him from his beloved security blanket. The busy, bossy, and ever-outrageous Lilly learns how to accept the arrival of her new attention-stealing brother in *Julius, the Baby of the World* (1990), and becomes the star of her own show in *Lilly's Purple Plastic Purse* (1996). Other mice titles include *Sheila Rae, the Brave* (1987) and *Chrysanthemum* (1991). Henkes is as eloquent with novels as he is with picture books; his middle-grade novels include *Words of Stone* (1992) and *Sun and Spoon* (1997).

HOBAN, RUSSELL [p. 165, American, b. 1925] is best known for his tales about Frances, the endearing little badger, which were inspired by watching his own children growing up. Every preschooler can identify with Frances's delaying tactics in *Bedtime for Frances* (1960), and every parent can appreciate the wisdom of the mother badger in *Bread and Jam for Frances* (1964). Hoban wrote five more Frances books before he turned to longer works of fiction, such as the children's novel *The Mouse and His Child* (1967) and the notable adult novel *Riddley Walker* (1980).

HURD, CLEMENT [p. 34, American, 1908–1988] is best known for his bold, bright illustrations, such as those he created for Margaret Wise Brown's *Goodnight Moon* (1947). Hurd and Brown also collaborated on many other cherished titles, including *The Runaway Bunny* (1942) and *The Little Brass Band* (1955). Hurd illustrated nearly fifty books that were written by his wife, Edith Thacher Hurd.

HUTCHINS, PAT [p. 103, British, b. 1942] made her picture-book debut in 1968 as the author and illustrator of *Rosie's Walk*, a clever, high-action story told with just thirty-two words. With their strong, distinctive illustrations set against clean white backgrounds and their simple, funny stories, her picture books are especially satisfying. *Titch* (1971) and its sequels speak to youngest siblings everywhere. *The Wind Blew* (1974) was awarded England's prestigious Kate Greenaway Medal.

JERAM, ANITA [p. 79, American, b. 1965] keeps a menagerie of creatures great and small, including toads, rats, cats, snakes, and lizards, from which she draws inspiration. Her love of animals is evident in her tender and joyous illustrations of the nutbrown hares in *Guess How Much I Love You* (1994) by Sam McBratney. Jeram has also illustrated books by Dick King-Smith, as well as her own *Daisy Dare* (1995) and *Birthday Happy, Contrary Mary* (1998).

KEATS, EZRA JACK [p. 42, American, 1916–1983] was a champion of the city and the children who live there. He had illustrated nearly a dozen picture books before he wrote and illustrated the Caldecott Medal winner *The Snowy Day* (1962). It was one of the very first picture books in which a child of color represents all children. Other titles featuring *The Snowy Day*'s Peter are *Whistle for Willie* (1964); *Peter's Chair* (1967); *Goggles!* (1969), a Caldecott Honor book; *Hi, Cat!* (1970); and *Pet Show* (1972).

KRAUS, ROBERT [p. 257, American, b. 1925] was a cartoonist for *The New Yorker* before he began writing and illustrating children's books in the 1950s. His ability to present early childhood experiences with humor and reassurance is displayed in *Whose Mouse Are You?* (1970), *Leo the Late Bloomer* (1971), *Milton the Early Riser* (1972), and *Owliver* (1974), all illustrated by Jose Aruego and Ariane Dewey.

LAWSON, ROBERT [p. 277, American, 1892–1957] had the distinction of being the only winner of both the Caldecott Medal for illustration (for *They Were Strong and Good* [1940], which he also wrote) and the Newbery Medal for writing (for *Rabbit Hill* [1944], which he also illustrated). It was his collaboration with Munro Leaf on *The Story of Ferdinand* in 1936 that introduced him to children's books and brought him international recognition. In 1939, with *Ben and Me*, the story of Benjamin Franklin as told by a mouse roommate, Lawson became a writer as well as an illustrator. He wrote and illustrated twenty books and illustrated forty-six more for other authors.

LEAF, MUNRO [p. 277, American, 1905–1976] wrote and illustrated nearly forty books, but he will be remembered forever as the author of *The Story of Ferdinand* (1936), the first American picture book to be labeled subversive. Banned in civil-war-torn Spain of the 1930s, burned in Nazi Germany, labeled in the United States as a promoter of both fascism *and* communism, and heralded throughout the world as a fable of pacifism, *The Story of Ferdinand* has calmly survived all kinds of "isms." It is a story with universal child appeal.

LIONNI, LEO [p. 23, Dutch-born American, b. 1910] was enjoying a distinguished career as an artist and graphic designer when, one day, to entertain his grandchildren, he tore up some yellow and blue pieces of paper and made up a story, which became his first book, *Little Blue and Little Yellow* (1959). He went on to create more than forty books for children, including four Caldecott Honor Books— *Inch by Inch* (1960), *Swimmy* (1963), *Frederick* (1967), and *Alexander and the Wind-Up Mouse* (1969). Lionni's stories address such universal topics as friendship, creativity, and cooperation.

LOBEL, ARNOLD [p. 48, American, 1933–1987] wrote and illustrated twenty-eight of his own books and illustrated over seventy for other authors. He is remembered for his warm and compassionate stories of friendship as exemplified by *Frog and Toad Are Friends* (1970), *Frog and Toad Together* (1972), *Frog and Toad All Year* (1976), and *Days with Frog and Toad* (1979). Excellent examples of his delightful sense of the absurd and fondness for clothing animals in Victorian dress can be seen in his Caldecott Medal winner, *Fables* (1980), and in *The Arnold Lobel Book of Mother Goose* (1986).

MARCELLINO, FRED [p. 293, American, b. 1939] excelled in book jacket illustration before turning to children's book illustration with Charles Perrault's *Puss in Boots* (1990), a Caldecott Honor Book. Other classics he has illustrated are Hans Christian Andersen's *The Steadfast Tin Soldier* (1992) and Edward Lear's *The Pelican Chorus and Other Nonsense* (1995).

MARSHALL, JAMES [p. 99, American, 1942–1992] was able in just a few lines to capture the hilarity and essence of his many memorable characters and to create a remarkable range of expression. Marshall is best known for his many collaborations with Harry Allard, such as the Miss Nelson books and their off-beat Stupid family books, as well as his own books about the special friendship between two hippos, George and Martha. He created seven of these stories, including *George and Martha* (1972), *George and Martha Encore* (1973), and *George and Martha Back in Town* (1984), and he received a Caldecott Honor for his fairy tale spoof *Goldilocks* (1988).

MARTIN, JR., BILL [p. 15, American, b. 1916] has written over 200 books for children. He has collaborated with writer John Archambault on nine books, including *Chicka Chicka Boom Boom* (1989), illustrated by Lois Ehlert. Martin's books are known for finding new and interesting ways to present early-learning concepts, as in *Brown Bear, Brown Bear, What Do You See?* (1983), illustrated by Eric Carle.

MAYER, MERCER [p. 72, American, b. 1943] began his career in 1967 with the publication of *A Boy, a Dog and a Frog*, the first in his series of wordless picture books. Since then he has authored and/or illustrated more than 100 children's books. He is widely known for *There's a Nightmare in My Closet* (1968) and the "Little Critter" series.

McBRATNEY, SAM [p. 79, British, b. 1943] has written more than fifty books for children, along with a dozen radio plays for adults and a prize-winning collection of adult short stories. Formerly a teacher, he now devotes himself full-time to writing. *Guess How Much I Love You* has remained a children's best-selling book ever since it was published in 1994.

McCLOSKEY, ROBERT [p. 55, American, b. 1914] wrote and illustrated eight books and illustrated another ten. He is best known for picture books, such as *Lentil* (1940); his Caldecott Medal winner, *Make Way for Ducklings* (1941); and *Blueberries for Sal* (1948), a Caldecott Honor Book. He also wrote funny stories for older readers; one of the best is *Homer Price* (1943). His settings and humor single him out as the first truly American picture-book creator. While he was working on *Make Way for Ducklings*, he shared his New York City apartment with ten mallards and their chicks to get his drawings "just right."

McKISSACK, PATRICIA C. [p. 67, American, b. 1944] grew up in a storytelling family in Tennessee, and she has continued this tradition as the author of *Flossie and the Fox* (1986), *Mirandy and Brother Wind* (1988), which won both a Caldecott Honor and the Coretta Scott King Award for Jerry Pinkney's illustrations, *A Million Fish . . . More or Less* (1992), *Ma Dear's Aprons* (1997), and her collection of ghost stories *The Dark-Thirty: Southern Tales of the Supernatural* (1992), a Newbery Honor Book and a Coretta Scott King Award winner. On her own and with her husband, Fredrick, she has also written many biographies for children about important African Americans.

MILNE, A. A. [p. 160, British, 1882–1956] wrote novels, short stories, poetry, and plays for adults, but it is incontestably his books about his son, Christopher Robin, and his stuffed animal friends that have brought the author everlasting fame. Both *Winnie-the-Pooh* (1926) and *The House at Pooh Corner* (1928) have captured the hearts of generations of children worldwide and made Winnie-the-Pooh a household name. Milne's *When We Were Very Young* (1924) and *Now We Are Six* (1927) endure as some of the most popular children's books of poetry ever published.

OXENBURY, HELEN [p. 96, British, b. 1938] felt a need for more books for her own children when they were toddlers and preschoolers and so became one of the first author-illustrators to design board books. Her many concept books, including *I Can, I Hear, I See,* and *I Touch* (all 1986), are representative of her characteristic warmth and gentle humor. Oxenbury has received many awards, including two Kate Greenaway Medals, and is the illustrator of Eugene Trivizas's parody *The Three Little Wolves and the Big Bad Pig* (1993).

PARISH, PEGGY [p. 235, American, 1927–1988], a pioneer in the genre of easy readers, is best known for her stories about Amelia Bedelia, the literal-minded housekeeper who just can't seem to get instructions right. Some of the favorite books about Amelia Bedelia are *Amelia Bedelia* (1963), *Teach Us, Amelia Bedelia* (1977), and *Amelia Bedelia Helps Out* (1979). Parish wrote close to fifty children's books, including *The Key to the Treasure* (1966), one of the first easy-to-read mysteries.

PIEŃKOWSKI, JAN [p. 198, Polish-born British, b. 1936] is known for his bold line drawings filled with highly charged colors and his black silhouette cutouts, like those appearing in "The Elves in the Shelves." Author as well as illustrator, Pieńkowski has created many concept books, such as *Numbers, Colors, Sizes,* and *Shapes* (all 1973), and innovative pop-up books. His first pop-up book, *Haunted House* (1979), was awarded the Kate Greenaway Medal.

RATHMANN, PEGGY [p. 133, American, b. 1953] creates unforgettable and delightful characters for the picture-book set. The sneaky apish protagonist of *Good Night, Gorilla* (1994), the precocious *Ruby the Copycat* (1991), and the helpful canine in the heartwarming partner story *Officer Buckle and Gloria* (1995), winner of the Caldecott Medal, have all been inspired by people (or animals) Rathmann has known.

REY, H. A. [p. 88, American, 1898–1977] created the most famous and most mischievous fictional monkey of all time, Curious George. Known in England as Zozo and in France as Fifi, the protagonist of *Curious George* (1941) became the subject of many subsequent books and has found his way into print in more than a dozen languages.

RISOM, OLE [p. 243, Danish-born American, b. 1919] is a picture-book art director who was responsible for many of the best mass-market books published in the United States after World War II. *I Am a Bunny* (1963) is one of the few books that bears his name, though he conceptualized many. He was Richard Scarry's collaborator and art director from 1958 until Scarry's death in 1994 and conceived and was in charge of Picturebacks, a Random House series of inexpensive paperback picture books.

SCARRY, RICHARD [p. 243, American, 1919–1994] was the creator of Huckle Cat, Lowly Worm, Mr. Frumble, and the whole cast of Busytown characters. For four decades children have learned about society through these characters and their structured world. His superlatively titled books, like *Richard Scarry's Best Word Book Ever* (1963) and *Richard Scarry's Biggest Word Book Ever!* (1985) (in an enormous trim size), are filled with hundreds of labeled objects and lessons about honesty, politeness, kindness, and other social skills.

SCHUTZER, DENA [p. 67, American, b. 1954] is the illustrator of seven books for children. Her vibrant, expressive oil paintings can be found in *A Million Fish . . . More or Less* (1992) by Patricia C. McKissack, her own *Polka and Dot* (1994), *Erin's Voyage* (1994) by John Frank, *The Hungry Little Boy* (1995) by Joan Blos, and *Three Kids Dreamin'* (1997) by Linda England, among others.

SCIESZKA, JON [p. 178, American, b. 1954] has collaborated with Lane Smith on a number of hilarious picture books for older readers, such as *The True Story of the Three Little Pigs* (1989), an amusing recasting of the story from the wolf's point of view; *The Stinky Cheese Man and Other Fairly Stupid Tales* (1992), a Caldecott Honor Book that turns nine fairy tales on their heads; *Math Curse* (1995), in which every event in a child's day becomes a math problem; and *Squids Will Be Squids* (1998).

SENDAK, MAURICE [p. 106, American, b. 1928] revolutionized children's literature by openly depicting the inner fantasies and fears of Max, tamer of monsters, in *Where the Wild Things Are* (1963), the Caldecott Medal winner. It was followed by the wonderfully surreal *In the Night Kitchen* (1970) and *Outside Over There* (1981). Sendak has written and/or illustrated over 100 books, including such favorites as Else Holmelund Minarik's "Little Bear" books, the four Nutshell Library books (1962)—*Pierre, Chicken Soup with Rice, One Was Johnny,* and *Alligators All Around*—and the philosophical *Higglety Pigglety Pop!* (1967).

SEUSS, DR. [p. 281, American, 1904–1991], whose real name was Theodor Seuss Geisel, wrote and illustrated his first children's book, *And to Think That I Saw It on Mulberry Street,* in 1937 and his last, *Oh, the Places You'll Go!,* in 1990. In between he created an additional forty-one books and is generally regarded as the most beloved author of children's books in America. He applied his joyous rhymes and inventive illustrations to honor the world's underdogs in stories such as *Horton Hears a Who!* (1954), *The Sneetches and Other Stories* (1961), and *The Lorax* (1971). Two of his books—*McElligot's Pool* (1947) and *Bartholomew and the Oobleck* (1949)—were Caldecott Honor Books, and in 1980 he was awarded the prestigious Laura Ingalls Wilder Award from the American Library Association for his body of work. But it was *The Cat in the Hat* (1957), which he wrote with just 223 words, that made the name Dr. Seuss synonymous with the fun of learning to read.

SHEPARD, ERNEST H. [p. 160, British, 1879–1976] was the illustrator of A. A. Milne's Winnie-the-Pooh books. He is equally well known for his delightful drawings for the 1931 edition of Kenneth Grahame's *The Wind in the Willows* and many other classics of children's literature.

SIEBEL, FRITZ [p. 235, Austrian-born American, 1913–1991] illustrated over a dozen books for children, including *A Fly Went By* (1958) by Mike McClintock, *Tell Me Some More* (1961) by Crosby Newell Bonsall, and *Amelia Bedelia* (1963), *Thank You, Amelia Bedelia* (1964), and *Amelia Bedelia and the Surprise Shower* (1966), all by Peggy Parish. His work in animated cartoons as the creator of "Mr. Clean" was seen by millions of television viewers.

SMITH, LANE [p. 178, American, b. 1959] has collaborated with Jon Scieszka on *The True Story of the Three Little Pigs* (1989) and *The Stinky Cheese Man and Other Fairly Stupid Tales* (1992), which received a Caldecott Honor Award, *Math Curse* (1995), and *Squids Will Be Squids* (1998). A lifelong admirer of Dr. Seuss, he brought life to *Hooray for Diffendoofer Day!* (1998), an original Seuss idea completed by children's poet Jack Prelutsky. His sophisticated, avant-garde style has helped expand the children's book audience to older children and adults.

STEIG, WILLIAM [p. 125, American, b. 1907] belonged to the elite corps of *The New Yorker* cartoonists for many years before coming to children's books at the age of sixty. Since then he has written and illustrated more than twenty books and illustrated eight written by others. He received the Caldecott Medal for *Sylvester and the Magic Pebble* (1969), a Caldecott Honor for *The Amazing Bone* (1976), and Newbery Honors for *Abel's Island* (1976) and *Doctor De Soto* (1982).

STEPTOE, JOHN [p. 149, American, 1950–1989] wrote and illustrated his first book, *Stevie* (1969), when he was just nineteen years old. This was followed by *Uptown* (1970) and *Train Ride* (1971), which formed a trilogy about the experience of black inner-city children and established his reputation. Two of his books, *The Story of Jumping Mouse: A Native American Legend* (1984) and *Mufaro's Beautiful Daughters: An African Tale* (1987), were Caldecott Honor Books. Steptoe wrote and illustrated eleven books and illustrated six others before he died at the young age of thirty-nine.

VIORST, JUDITH [p. 86, American, b. 1931], poet and author, sensitively and humorously weaves compelling stories for children around common childhood problems. She is best known for her books about the trials and tribulations of a boy named Alexander, including *Alexander and the Terrible, Horrible, No Good, Very Bad Day* (1972), *Alexander Who Used to Be Rich Last Sunday* (1978), and *Alexander, Who's Not (Do You Hear Me? I Mean It!) Going to Move* (1995). *The Tenth Good Thing About Barney* (1971), a story about a cat who has died, has become a classic in helping children deal with grief.

WELLS, ROSEMARY [p. 230, American, b. 1943] excels at capturing the world of preschool children through her humorous stories and appealing pictures of animals. Realistic—often mildly rebellious—interaction between siblings and parents is wonderfully shown in her Max and Ruby board books, *Benjamin and Tulip* (1973), and *Noisy Nora* (1973). *First Tomato*, part of her *Voyage to the Bunny Planet* trilogy (1992), is a fantasy journey to a place where bad days are set right. She is also the illustrator of the sumptuous *My Very First Mother Goose* (1996), edited by Iona Opie, and has written several notable young adult novels.

WILLIAMS, GARTH [p. 165, American, 1912–1997] illustrated more than eighty picture books, beginning with E. B. White's *Stuart Little* (1945). His delightful illustrations for Margaret Wise Brown's *Little Fur Family* (1946) soon followed, setting in motion a long collaboration that would result in eleven books. Williams is also well known for illustrating White's *Charlotte's Web* (1952), Laura Ingalls Wilder's "Little House" books, and Russell Hoban's *Bedtime for Frances* (1960).

WILLIAMS, VERA B. [p. 27, American, b. 1927] is the author-illustrator of many award-winning picture books, such as her two Caldecott Honor Books, *A Chair for My Mother* (1982) and *"More More More," Said the Baby: Three Love Stories* (1990). Her books portray strong female characters and loving family relations and are frequently set in multicultural communities with black, Asian, or Hispanic children as the protagonists. These joyous, energetic picture books that speak to every child include *Three Days on a River in a Red Canoe* (1981), *Music, Music for Everyone* (1984), and *Lucky Song* (1997).

ZION, GENE [p. 249, American, 1913–1975] collaborated with his then wife Margaret Bloy Graham on more than a dozen enchanting picture books. The first of these, *All Falling Down* (1951), established Zion's witty and playful, though reassuring, tone through a lively presentation of things that fall down and things that don't (a baby in his father's arms). *Harry the Dirty Dog* (1956) was the first in the forever popular series of stories that includes *No Roses for Harry!* (1958), *Harry and the Lady Next Door* (1960), and *Harry by the Sea* (1965).

GUIDE TO READING AGES

YOUNGEST

YOUNGER

YOUNG

INDEX OF TITLES, AUTHORS, AND ILLUSTRATORS

ACKNOWLEDGMENTS

Grateful acknowledgment is made to the following
for permission to reprint previously published material:

Alexander and the Terrible, Horrible, No Good, Very Bad Day by Judith Viorst, illustrated by Ray Cruz. Text copyright © 1972 by Judith Viorst. Illustrations copyright © 1972 by Ray Cruz. Reprinted by permission of Simon & Schuster Children's Publishing Division.

Amelia Bedelia by Peggy Parish, illustrated by Fritz Siebel. Text copyright © 1963 by Peggy Parish. Copyright © renewed 1992. Illustrations copyright © 1963 by Fritz Siebel. Copyright © renewed 1992. Reprinted by permission of HarperCollins Publishers.

Bedtime for Frances by Russell Hoban, illustrated by Garth Williams. Text copyright © 1960 by Russell C. Hoban. Copyright © renewed 1988 by Russell C. Hoban. Illustrations copyright © 1960, 1996 by Garth Williams. Copyright © renewed 1988 by Garth Williams. Reprinted by permission of HarperCollins Publishers.

The Berenstain Bears and the Spooky Old Tree by Stanley and Janice Berenstain. Copyright © 1978 by Stanley and Janice Berenstain. Reprinted by permission of Random House, Inc.

A Boy, a Dog and a Frog by Mercer Mayer. Copyright © 1967 by Mercer Mayer. Reprinted by permission of Penguin Putnam, Inc.

The Cat Club by Esther Averill. Copyright © 1944 by Esther Averill. Copyright © renewed 1972 by Esther Averill. Reprinted by permission of HarperCollins Publishers.

A Chair for My Mother by Vera B. Williams. Copyright © 1982 by Vera B. Williams. By permission of Greenwillow Books, a division of William Morrow & Company, Inc.

Chicka Chicka Boom Boom by Bill Martin, Jr., and John Archambault, illustrated by Lois Ehlert. Text copyright © 1989 by Bill Martin, Jr., and John Archambault. Illustrations copyright © 1989 by Lois Ehlert. Reprinted by permission of Simon & Schuster Children's Publishing Division.

Curious George by H. A. Rey. Copyright © 1941 and © renewed 1969 by Margaret E. Rey. Copyright assigned to Houghton Mifflin Company in 1993. Reprinted by permission of Houghton Mifflin Company. All rights reserved.

D.W. the Picky Eater by Marc Brown. Copyright © 1995 by Marc Brown. Reprinted by permission of Little, Brown and Company, Inc.

"The Elves in the Shelves" from *A Necklace of Raindrops* by Joan Aiken, illustrated by Jan Pieńkowski. Text copyright © 1968 by Joan Aiken. Text reprinted by permission of Brandt & Brandt Literary Agents, Inc. Illustrations copyright © Jonathan Cape. Illustrations reprinted by permission of Random House UK Limited.

First Tomato by Rosemary Wells. Copyright © 1992 by Rosemary Wells. Reprinted by permission of Penguin Putnam, Inc.

Freight Train by Donald Crews. Copyright © 1978 by Donald Crews. By permission of Greenwillow Books, a division of William Morrow & Company, Inc.

Good Night, Gorilla by Peggy Rathmann. Copyright © 1994 by Peggy Rathmann. Reprinted by permission of Penguin Putnam, Inc.

Goodnight Moon by Margaret Wise Brown, illustrated by Clement Hurd. Copyright © 1947 by Harper & Row, Publishers, Inc. Text copyright © renewed 1975 by Roberta Brown Rauch. Illustrations copyright © renewed 1975 by Edith T. Hurd, Clement Hurd, John Thacher Hurd, and George Hellyer, as Trustees of the Edith T. Hurd and Clement Hurd 1982 Trust. Reprinted by permission of HarperCollins Publishers.

Guess How Much I Love You by Sam McBratney, illustrated by Anita Jeram. Text copyright © 1994 by Sam McBratney. Illustrations copyright © 1994 by Anita Jeram. Published by Candlewick Press, Cambridge, Mass. Reprinted by permission of Walker Books Ltd., London.

Harry the Dirty Dog by Gene Zion, illustrated by Margaret Bloy Graham. Text copyright © 1956 by Eugene Zion. Copyright © renewed 1984 by Ruth Zion Frischer. Illustrations copyright © 1956 by Margaret Bloy Graham. Copyright © renewed 1984 by Margaret Bloy Graham. Reprinted by permission of HarperCollins Publishers.

I Am a Bunny by Ole Risom, illustrated by Richard Scarry. Copyright © 1963 Golden Books Publishing Company, Inc. Used by permission.

I See; I Hear; I Touch by Helen Oxenbury. Copyright © 1985 Helen Oxenbury. Published by Candlewick Press, Cambridge, Mass. Reprinted by permission of Walker Books Ltd., London.

"In Which Pooh Goes Visiting..." from *Winnie-the-Pooh* by A. A. Milne, illustrated by Ernest H. Shepard. Text copyright © 1926 by E. P. Dutton & Co., Inc. Copyright © renewed 1954 by A. A. Milne. Reprinted by permission of Penguin Putnam, Inc.

"The Letter" from *Frog and Toad Are Friends* by Arnold Lobel. Copyright © 1970 by Arnold Lobel. Reprinted by permission of HarperCollins Publishers.

Madeline by Ludwig Bemelmans. Copyright © 1939 by Ludwig Bemelmans. Copyright © renewed 1967 by Madeline Bemelmans and Barbara Bemelmans Marciano. Reprinted by permission of Penguin Putnam, Inc.

Make Way for Ducklings by Robert McCloskey. Copyright © 1941 by Robert McCloskey. Copyright © renewed 1969 by Robert McCloskey. Reprinted by permission of Penguin Putnam, Inc.

Mike Mulligan and His Steam Shovel by Virginia Lee Burton. Copyright © 1939 by Virginia Lee Burton. Copyright © renewed 1967 by Virginia Lee Demetrios. Reprinted by permission of Houghton Mifflin Company. All rights reserved.

A Million Fish...More or Less by Patricia C. McKissack, illustrated by Dena Schutzer. Text copyright © 1992 by Patricia C. McKissack. Illustrations copyright © 1992 by Dena Schutzer. Reprinted by permission of Alfred A. Knopf, Inc.

Millions of Cats by Wanda Gág. Copyright © 1928 by Coward, McCann, Inc. Copyright © renewed 1956 by Robert Janssen. Reprinted by permission of Penguin Putnam, Inc.

Miss Nelson Is Missing! by Harry Allard, illustrated by James Marshall. Text copyright © 1977 by Harry Allard. Illustrations copyright © 1977 by James Marshall. Reprinted by permission of Houghton Mifflin Company. All rights reserved.

Owen by Kevin Henkes. Copyright © 1993 by Kevin Henkes. By permission of Greenwillow Books, a division of William Morrow & Company, Inc.

Petunia by Roger Duvoisin. Copyright © 1950 and renewed 1978 by Roger Duvoisin. Reprinted by permission of Alfred A. Knopf, Inc.

"The Sneetches" from *The Sneetches and Other Stories* by Dr. Seuss. TM and copyright © 1961 and renewed 1989 by Dr. Seuss Enterprises, L.P. Reprinted by permission of Random House, Inc.

The Snowy Day by Ezra Jack Keats. Copyright © 1962 by Ezra Jack Keats. Copyright © renewed 1990 by Martin Pope. Reprinted by permission of Penguin Putnam, Inc.

Stellaluna by Janell Cannon. Copyright © 1993 by Janell Cannon. Reprinted by arrangement with Harcourt Brace & Company.

Stevie by John Steptoe. Copyright © 1969 by John L. Steptoe. Copyright © renewed 1997 by the Estate of John L. Steptoe. Reprinted by permission of HarperCollins Publishers and the Estate of John L. Steptoe.

"The Stinky Cheese Man" from *The Stinky Cheese Man and Other Fairly Stupid Tales* by Jon Scieszka, illustrated by Lane Smith. Text copyright © 1992 by Jon Scieszka. Illustrations copyright © 1992 by Lane Smith. Reprinted by permission of Penguin Putnam, Inc.

The Story of Babar by Jean de Brunhoff. Copyright © 1933 and renewed 1961 by Random House, Inc. Reprinted by permission of Random House, Inc.

The Story of Ferdinand by Munro Leaf, illustrated by Robert Lawson. Text copyright © 1936 by Munro Leaf. Illustrations copyright © 1936 by Robert Lawson. Copyright © renewed 1964 by Munro Leaf and John W. Boyd. Reprinted by permission of Penguin Putnam, Inc.

The Story of Little Babaji by Helen Bannerman, illustrated by Fred Marcellino. Copyright © 1996 by Fred Marcellino. Reprinted by arrangement with Michael de Capua Books/HarperCollins Publishers.

Swimmy by Leo Lionni. Copyright © 1963 and renewed 1991 by Leo Lionni. Reprinted by permission of Pantheon Books, a division of Random House, Inc.

Sylvester and the Magic Pebble by William Steig. Copyright © 1969 by William Steig. Copyright © renewed 1997 by William Steig. Reprinted by permission of Simon & Schuster Children's Publishing Division.

Ten, Nine, Eight by Molly Bang. Copyright © 1983 by Molly Garrett Bang. By permission of Greenwillow Books, a division of William Morrow & Company, Inc.

Titch by Pat Hutchins. Copyright © 1971 by Pat Hutchins. Reprinted by permission of Simon & Schuster Children's Publishing Division.

The Tub People by Pam Conrad, illustrated by Richard Egielski. Text copyright © 1989 by Pam Conrad. Illustrations copyright © 1989 by Richard Egielski. Reprinted by permission of HarperCollins Publishers.

Where the Wild Things Are by Maurice Sendak. Copyright © 1963 by Maurice Sendak. Copyright © renewed 1991 by Maurice Sendak. Reprinted by arrangement with Michael de Capua Books/HarperCollins Publishers.

Whose Mouse Are You? by Robert Kraus, illustrated by Jose Aruego. Text copyright © 1970 by Robert Kraus. Illustrations copyright © 1970 by Jose Aruego. Reprinted by permission of Simon & Schuster Children's Publishing Division.